"Gabriel Cohen is as brave as he is talented, not just because he delves fearlessly into the difficult topics of racism and gentrification, but because he inhabits the hearts and minds of such a disparate cast of characters."

—LISA SELIN DAVIS, AUTHOR OF *BELLY*

Praise for *Red Hook*:

"This first effort . . . is better than promising (may the gods take note): it is accomplished. [A] fine novel deserving of attention."

—*PUBLISHERS WEEKLY*

"I really enjoyed *Red Hook*—a beautifully written, atmospheric book with strong characters and an interesting plot."

—PHILLIP LOPATE

"This compelling first novel offers an amazingly deft mystery of character."

—*BOOKLIST*

BOOMBOX

GABRIEL COHEN

BOOMBOX

A NOVEL

ACADEMY

CHICAGO

Published in 2007 by
Academy Chicago Publishers
363 West Erie Street
Chicago, Illinois 60610

© 2007 by Gabriel Cohen

Library of Congress Cataloging-in-Publication Data on file with the publisher.

Released from the basement, the dog pads out into the courtyard, head swaying from side to side as it follows invisible wild tendrils of scent. It pauses to shake the summer rain off its shoulders, enjoying the stretch of muscle over bone.

A scrappling of claws in the chain link fence. The orange cat chins itself up.

The dog bays, snaps, and leaps, twisting its torso in its eagerness. Falls short.

The cat perches on the fence, turning its head away in an elaborate show of indifference. Gingerly, it extends one paw; changes its mind. It peruses the corner of the next yard until it finds just the right place to drop down.

The dog barks mournfully, first at the disappearing cat, then at the unjust world.

Two yards over, the cat rushes a cherry tree and a flock of sparrows flashes into the air like leaves suddenly granted the power of flight. Over the roofs of the courtyard; gone.

CHAPTER ONE

CAROL FASONE

"Milosz?"

Carol Fasone stands in her front hall, head cocked to one side, listening. A grocery bag weighs one shoulder down; the other is raised to keep her purse from sliding off. She calls out again, the sound muted by the worn carpet. No answer.

She hurries down the hallway into the kitchen and sets the bag on the counter. The sun slants through the windows; there's still an hour of light left on this warm Brooklyn day. Carol pauses, tugged by a pang of conscience—she should be making her husband's dinner now—but she stows the perishables in the fridge and dashes upstairs, her lanky legs taking the steps two at a time.

In the bedroom, breathless, she doesn't even pause to take off her shoes: just pulls the skirt of her work suit down over the big pink and white sneakers. As she wriggles into an old tracksuit, a harsh voice calls from upstairs.

"Carrie? Is that you?"

She smiles to herself. "No, Ma, it's a burglar."

A jagged cough from on high. "Very funny."

Carol looks longingly out the window toward her garden, but takes a minute to go upstairs, where her mother lies smoking in her musty bedroom, her plump body encased in an ancient silk dress with a purple beetle sheen.

"You gonna have dinner with us?" Carol asks.

Her mother plucks a shred of tobacco from her lip. She squints. "Where's that husband of yours?"

"I think . . . he's at the library," Carol answers, guilty about the lie, then mad at herself for this reaction. Why should she have to protect her husband from this sour old woman? Her mother looks down on Milosz for going to school while Carol supports him, but soon he'll have his engineering degree—he'll bring home so much money she'll be silenced for good.

"Library closes at six, Wednesday nights." The old lady doesn't miss a trick.

Carol finds her good mood dropping away. "Jesus, Ma, all I asked is if you wanted to eat with us."

"Please, honey, don't take the name of our Lord—"

Carol groans and turns on her heel. "I'm gonna start cooking soon. You come if you want."

"I saw you out on the front stoop," her mother says coyly, as if revealing some big secret.

Carol pauses in the doorway. "What, are you spying on me now?"

"Why do you waste your time talking to that woman?"

"*That woman*. Do you mean our neighbor? *Grace?*"

Her mother leans over and stubs out her cigarette. "Remember our house in Bay Ridge? What a lovely neighborhood that was. So clean, so quiet . . ."

"So white," Carol finishes for her. "Ma, you are such a bigot."

"I don't have anything against those people." Her mother raises her palms in a show of innocence.

"Right—'As long as they keep to their own neighborhoods.'"

Her mother shrugs. "What's wrong with that? It makes every-body happier."

"If I kept to my own neighborhood, I'd never have found Milosz. I'd be single and lonely. I guess that would make *you* happy."

Her mother looks pained. "Honey, I only wish you the best. You know that, don't you?"

Just when Carol feels her heart softening, the old woman can't resist adding, "Although I can't see why someone from the neighbor-hood wasn't good enough for you."

"Someone Italian," Carol translates. "Ma, why can't you just leave him alone?" She groans. "You can make your own damn dinner."

Unfazed, her mother shrugs again. "I'll heat up some Weight Watchers." She coughs; lights another cigarette. "He's kind of late, isn't he?"

Carol starts to worry.

* * *

Hoping to regain some peace of mind, she steps out into her back-yard. The roses are still in bloom, masses of dusky wine blossoms, but they're browning at the edges. There won't be many days left before frost robs the garden of its green. Most evenings it's already too cool to barbecue.

Carol pulls out a pack of Winstons. Normally she tries to smoke only during work, spacing out her breaks as markers toward five o'clock. Rewards for each hour at the keyboard, foot shifting over the pedal of the Dictaphone. *What the hell?* she thinks now. Why not take a reward for making it through another day?

An orange cat descends a neighbor's fire escape, placing each paw carefully before it. Overhead, the mimosa tree has already shed most of its curling leaves, though a host of pods remain, translucent in the sun, revealing the dark seeds inside. Sometimes the pods remind Carol of a candy she used to buy at the five-and-dime, bright sugar bumps stuck to a roll of paper, but this afternoon a different association jumps to mind. They droop down from the branches like little brown crucifixes. *Calvary.* She shivers at the image, shakes her head, thinking: This is what too many years of Catholic school will do to a person.

Over the rooftops, a distant jet glints in the sun, a tiny flying thermometer.

Carol sees movement through the greenery of the court: it's a young blonde woman, one of the new neighbors. They've been here a couple of months, but so far Carol has learned nothing about them. The woman stoops to weed the border of her garden. She keeps to herself.

Carol treads carefully among her own plants—red raspberry, elderberry, forsythia—stooping to pick up the droppings of the mimosa tree. She plucks a leaf from the monarda plant, crushes it between her fingers, raises them to inhale the sharp scent: bee balm. So many flowers, so many plants in the world. In her spare time, she likes to read gardening catalogs, in part just to enjoy the names. Alchemilla—*Lady's mantle*. Draconicum—*Leopard's bane*. Catananche—*Cupid's dart*. Dicentra—*Bleeding heart*.

Carol attends to her own weeding. Soon she feels a familiar ache in her spine—being tall is a disadvantage when it comes to gardening. At thirty-nine she's not as flexible as she used to be. She rests, leaning with a hand against a tree trunk covered in a scaly suit of ivy.

Music erupts across the courtyard, angry chanting over a thumping bass beat, coming from Jamel Wilson's yard. The boy comes out holding a small boombox. Carol frowns. She remembers when Jamel was younger, a funny kid who used to build forts in the dirt and hum to himself. One spring when he was eight or nine he even showed an interest in gardening, and—despite her mother's distrust of black people—she invited him over to teach him a few things. She grins: once she told him why she was spreading horse manure around the rose bushes, and the next day she overheard him explaining to a friend that it was important to put out "horse remover." Now, though, he's turning into a big sullen teenager, slouching around in droopy jeans, anxious to impress his buddies from the projects around the corner. When she passes him on the street these days he can barely bring himself to mutter hello.

After several minutes he goes back inside, leaving the courtyard quiet again. A bright yellow leaf somersaults down. In a couple of weeks the trees upstate will reach their fall peak. She hopes Milosz will agree to drive up along the Palisades Parkway, have a picnic to celebrate his new permanent resident status. As soon as the papers come through.

It's been three years now that she's had someone to share plans with.

She sneaks a look at her watch. Milosz *is* late. She catches herself worrying, then scowls up at her mother's window. A marriage is based on trust.

She tugs a weed from the base of a small plaster Virgin Mary that her husband gave her when they first met.

It all started when her mother offered to pay for a shared trip, a church pilgrimage to Medjugorje, the shrine in Bosnia where a group of children had seen a vision of the Madonna. On chartered planes, a train, a bus, they sat in a fog of cigarette smoke listening to a bunch of old women comparing their arthritis, bursitis, cancers. A tumor the size of a grapefruit. Twenty-five hours into the trip, as they motored up and down mountains, past patchworks of tobacco fields and vineyards, past houses with red-tiled roofs, Carol wondered why she had agreed to come.

A metal cross marked the hilltop where the children had seen their vision. Plastic roses were tucked into the pile of rocks around the base, along with candles and photos and rain-stained letters pleading for the Virgin's help. After, Carol's mother leaned against her as they walked down the dirt path leading away from the hill, past thorn bushes and brambles and scrawny goats, the old woman so teary-eyed that Carol couldn't help feeling a lump rise in her own throat.

Later, she waited for her mother outside a little village church. Purple clouds roiled over a darker purple mountain. Carol perched on a stone wall beside a field of tulips swaying in the breeze. Beautiful flowers.

A man sat on the end of the wall. He was thin and sunken-chested, but handsome, with a soccer player's cabled muscles. Carol shyly watched him roll a cigarette.

She looked away, but he said something to her in Yugoslavian.

"Sorry, I don't speak your language."

He drew a lungful of smoke, then repeated his comment in English. "Excuse me. I say, Why you are not in the Mass?" The question posed in a neutral, friendly way.

Something about him made her let down her guard.

"I could ask you the same question," she replied.

He nodded. "Very true. I wait for my mother. She is the one who is the great"—he struggled for the word—

"Believer?"

He grinned. "Yes. *Bihliver.*"

They talked until the sun set and bats flitted overhead into the light of a streetlamp. He asked about New York, about her house, her job, what she liked to do in the evenings—she couldn't remember the last time she had talked to a man so interested in her. And he spoke of things American—Bruce Willis and Calvin Klein—with a reverence she found touching.

They spent the next two days together under their mothers' suspicious eyes. He squired her around to Medjugorje's meager sites of interest, talking gravely about the political situation in his homeland. He took her and her mother out to dinner on their last night, and gave Carol a lingering kiss after her mother finally went off to bed. She was stunned. Such a good-looking man, interested in *her*.

The next morning, in the street outside her hotel, he brought forth a heavy wrapped bundle, handed it to her, and left.

While her mother packed in another room, Carol read a carefully lettered note: *Perhaps this is not most appropriat sovenir, but I hope you will remembr the special time we had in Medjugorje. I will writ to you. Love, Milosz.* She uncovered the bundle and found this statue of the Madonna that now stands watch in her garden.

A muffled cough sounds from a second floor window. As it turned out, the pilgrimage did nothing to help her mother's emphysema, although it did result in a miracle: Carol bucked all the horrendous statistics about older single women and found herself a husband. After a year of passionate letters and two short visits, they were married in a Brooklyn church.

She stands and approaches the statue. Made self-conscious by the neighbors—and by the uncertainty of her own faith—she genuflects in mind only. *Thank you for these blessings. Thank you for Milosz. Thank you.*

Across the court, the door to a shed swings open. Carol sees Grace's placid round brown face. She gives her neighbor a minute to survey her garden, enjoy a moment of solitude. Suddenly the cat rushes up the chain-link fence separating the yards. Startled, Grace looks up, sees her neighbor and laughs. They move toward the fence like farmers coming together over a stone wall.

"It's a beautiful evening," Grace says in her lilting Barbados accent.

"I can't complain."

"Your roses are still going strong."

Carol contemplates her garden. "I'm thinking of moving the azaleas farther out next spring. Maybe they'll do better with more sun." Her house, on the southern side of the courtyard, blocks a lot of the light.

"Makes sense," Grace says. "I see your little experiment turned out well." She points to an amaranth, its flowers a shade between magenta and plum; Carol had nursed it from a cutting she took over a fence on Warren Street.

They spend five minutes in easy conversation about the recent weather (too cloudy), the squirrels (too bothersome), the cherry tomatoes (so sweet this year).

Carol touches the leaves of a plant growing in the shade of the fence. "I don't recognize this one. Do you think it's a weed?"

Grace shrugs. "Leave it alone and see what it does."

Carol nods. Good advice, calm and steady like her gardening friend.

The trilling of a phone. "That's me," Grace says.

Carol sighs. "I should go in and start dinner." She looks at her watch. Maybe Milosz stayed late talking to one of his teachers.

She stands at the fence for a moment longer, watching her neighbor hurry down the flagstone path into her shed. A moment later Grace appears in her kitchen window and Carol pictures the bright, airy room: its many plants, its polished butcher block counters, the collection of West Indian pottery lined up over the stove. She has shared many cups of tea there. With her mother the way she is about black people, though, she has rarely been able to invite her neighbor into her own home. They don't talk about it; Grace just seems to understand.

The tarpaulin of dusk settles over the yard. Above, the setting sun has caught the underside of a fragmented train of clouds; silky stretched-out filaments flare fantastically in the last light. Carol remembers a saying of her late father's: *Mackerel sky and mares' tails/ Make sailors put up tall sails*. A change in the weather is on the way.

She takes one last look around the courtyard, breathes deep of the plant-scented air. Evening closes in, trees silhouetted against a dim pearly sky. Across the way, windows glow orange and warm in the mauve façades of the houses, and clothes on a line sway in the breeze like tired waltzers.

And then she hears the front gate creaking open. Milosz. She turns toward the house and her mother with a look that says *So there, you old bat.*

CHAPTER TWO

MITCHELL BRETT

STANDING WITH HIS HANDS ON HIS HIPS LIKE A RATHER SELF-conscious country squire, Mitchell Brett surveys his new backyard. The backs of the adjoining brick houses are painted beige or cream or gray; their gardens combine to form a rectangular court in the center of the block. His yard is forty feet long by twenty feet wide, separated from the others by a chain-link fence. Over one side drapes a trail of impossibly bright roses, a shock of magenta in this oasis of green. A picnic table rests at the far end, next to the neighbor's squat fig tree, its broad leaves rounded like patterns for a fat person's glove. Up in the tree, sparrows chirp aggressive single notes—Brooklyn birds seem too tough to actually sing. Beyond the block, a distant swirl of traffic, voices, sirens. Every now and then a plane slowly tears the sky over-head, La Guardia Airport bound.

In a corner of the garden his wife waters her roses; a band holds her fine blonde hair back from her pale, impassive face. Two months after moving here Kristin still grouses about living in Brooklyn, but at least she seems to enjoy the garden. It's what sold them on the place: the quiet, the bees hovering over the flowers, the old metal swing-chair.

She bends to gather up some dead leaves, her long legs stretching. Mitchell watches the way her sweatpants hang over her firm behind and feels an idle swelling in his groin.

"Could you do something for me?" she asks.

"I believe I could."

She turns to her garden, missing his lustful Groucho Marx impression. "I need to protect these basil plants from the squirrels. Would you make some sort of a tent out of chicken wire?"

"I'll go to the hardware store after work tomorrow."

Cherry tomatoes infiltrate the fence from a stunning garden next door, kept by a middle-aged West Indian woman who has told them that they are free to gather any of the crop that reaches their side. Two yards down, a daydreamy black teenager sometimes emerges with an ax and chops at a fallen log. Once or twice he has brought out a boombox and played music that set Mitchell's teeth on edge—gangster rap, he believes it's called, angry rhymes filled with curses and threats—but as long as it doesn't happen often, he supposes that he can tolerate it. Across the court a big, gawky white woman and her skinny husband, who speaks with some sort of Slavic accent, sometimes step out onto their deck in the evenings to enjoy a beer.

This, Mitchell reflects, is what former Mayor Dinkins liked to call "the urban mosaic," people of all colors renovating neighborhoods and living together in harmony. Almost. Somewhere in the facing row of houses, a woman with a powerful voice begins singing scales, over and over. "Keep it down, goddamnit!" someone yells from several houses away. Mitchell, not a big fan of opera himself, grins.

The tranquility of the court is not perfect. He has noticed that the "bees" are actually yellow jackets—they're forming a mud nest in the corner of the back doorframe. And he has become aware of the tops of the Wysocki Houses, a city housing project, rising over the far end of the court like giant red hives. At dusk, he stands in the yard to watch the lights flicking on in the towers, squares of yellow and orange and red. He didn't pay much attention to those buildings when he and his wife first moved in—they rushed into the signing because they were so relieved to find an affordable house this close to Manhattan.

As they lie in bed at night, the trilling of crickets is overwhelmed by Jeeps with giant stereo speakers, throbbing rhythms overlaid with angry black voices. In the velvety hours of the early morning he sometimes wakes to hear someone foraging for returnable bottles in the trash barrel out front, or a Hispanic couple conducting a bitter traveling marital spat.

* * *

At noon Sunday, he lies stretched out on the new sofa in the living room, the *Times* tented over his stomach. Kristin sits in an armchair staring off into space with a hollow, haunted look that spells trouble for the last precious hours of the weekend.

When they first met she had been sassy and funny, but a year of marriage has revealed an unpredictable, moody side. When she gets like this, sometimes he wonders if he hasn't made a mistake—if he didn't rush into marriage because of pressure to fit in, to do what all his friends seemed to be doing.

"Hey, why don't we go for a walk?" he says. "Check out the new neighborhood a little?"

She pushes a wisp of hair out of her face and gazes blankly at him. Uh oh. But then she brightens and gets up. She has always been athletic—maybe she just misses her morning run around the reservoir in Central Park.

They step out onto the front stoop. Two doors down, the black teenager is sitting with some friends, a big gangly guy and a short girl with orange hair. Mitchell thinks of waving in a neighborly fashion, but changes his mind; he'll look foolish if they don't respond.

Out on the sidewalk he's faced with a decision: right or left?

"Let's go this way," he says, turning away from the housing projects. He and his wife walk past Court Street, where they're not exploring their new neighborhood at all, but the one next to it, one of the fancy areas they couldn't afford.

Kristin perks up. The October day is crisp and Cobble Hill is trim and genteel, each home perfectly kept. Mitchell pauses to point out a majestic door with a brass lion's-head knocker. Kristin glances at a parlor window, attracted by the lace curtains, the violets on the sill.

She smiles and turns to him. "Soon we'll have a house like this." They've told each other that this move is temporary, until they can

afford a better place, maybe in Brooklyn Heights. She takes his hand
and they walk on.

The hill of Cobble Hill becomes apparent: the street slopes down
for five or six blocks until, framed between the rows of houses, Mitchell sees the gray East River. A long barge slides by, trailing a ripple
of white foam. And then somehow—he's powerless to stop it—the
afternoon itself begins to tilt away from him.

"If you could live in any house on this street, which would it be?"
he asks.

Kristin squints at each one as they stroll by. She stops in front of a
Victorian brownstone with a bay window and ornate cornices.

"*This* one?" he says.

"Why, don't you like it?"

He shrugs. He doesn't, but is not eager to open a new door of difference between them.

"Which one would you pick?" she asks.

He points to a Federalist townhouse, admiring its wooden shutters
and clean, simple lines.

"You've got to be kidding," she says. "This looks so *Upper East
Side.*"

What's wrong with that? he wants to ask—that's where he grew up,
after all. Someday they'll be able to afford their dream house, only
now it appears that she has a different dream altogether. How are they
going to settle that? They walk three blocks in silence.

"Are you pissed about something?" she says.

A moody sigh is his only response.

"If you're upset, why don't you just say so? I was talking to Dr.
Simon about this just last Wednesday—"

Six months in therapy and her shrink looms larger in her life than
he does. His wife has suggested that he try some therapy of his own,
but Mitchell resists. He doesn't feel any need to reveal his deep dark
secrets to a stranger. Not that he has any, really—his family was nor-
mal enough. No child abuse, no alcoholism. There was that time in
ninth grade that he and Tad Hasselbeck jerked off in his dad's den,
but they didn't touch each other, and besides, Cindy Slocombe was

there—she had dared them to do it, so it certainly wasn't a gay thing. Why would he want to pay someone to talk about crap like that?

"So what did she say?" He can't resist asking: maybe her shrink really does know what's happening between him and his wife. Maybe Dr. Simon knows more about it than he does.

Kristin shrugs. "She said you don't communicate enough."

He knows that it would be a good idea to say something at this point, something personal and sincerely felt. They continue on toward the river in silence.

As he passes an old brick apartment building, he glances into the lobby, right into a memory from when he was twelve. He had stood in the much more impressive lobby of a Park Avenue building, watching a moving company carry out his family's furniture. The leather-topped desk from his father's den. An ottoman covered in pale green silk. He barely understood what was happening; his father had been caught up in an insider trading scandal. Back then such activities were considered a mark of dishonor—that was before a new era brought them an almost sexual aura of power and intrigue. Mitchell's friends, the doormen, stood and watched the parade, Melton with his snow-white hair, Domingo with his fascinating caterpillar of a moustache. Mitchell's father approached the front door. For decades prior to that instant the doormen would have jumped forward to open it, but this time—putting the lie to all those years of cheerful greetings, quick nods of respect—they simply looked away. It was just his father's money they had respected. As his father pulled the door open himself Mitchell had reddened with shame.

"What are you doing?" calls Kristin, stopping to look back at him.

He blinks, turns from the empty entranceway, and jogs to catch up.

At the edge of the neighborhood, they come out onto Hicks Street, a broad boulevard running toward Brooklyn Heights and Red Hook. The scene would have been much the same during the previous century: old brick buildings, quaint church steeples, rusty water towers. Brooklyn, a humble plain of brick and stone.

Mitchell and his wife walk on, crossing a walkway over a stalled river of cars—the Brooklyn Queens Expressway—before they reach a spectacular view of Manhattan across the East River. The skyline is dominated by the shocking recent absence of the World Trade Center. The river slides past, a moat between their past and present lives. The sun shines on the water. It was Mitchell's idea to move here; he prays he made the right choice, that this will be the start of a new life for them.

Out of the blue, his wife leans over and kisses his cheek. He raises his eyebrows in surprise and gratitude.

* * *

Taking a different route home, they round a corner and discover an immaculate little park with iron railings, freshly planted trees, a fountain. And kids. Kids all over the place, crawling, skipping, twirling, laughing.

Let's go for a walk. Great idea, he thinks. For the past year he and his wife have been trying to conceive a child. During their honeymoon they drank a bottle of champagne and toasted their disposal of her diaphragm. He had felt sure she'd get pregnant that same night.

There was an article in the *Times* recently about how sperm counts are declining around the world. Another in *Newsweek* about the effect of beef hormones on human estrogen levels. Finally he and his wife have started talking about fertility clinics, even adoption.

A munchkin wearing a multicolored Peruvian knit cap motors jerkily out of the front gate, straight toward Kristin. The kid's mother runs up and scoops him onto her shoulder, scolding him. She gives them an apologetic grin: *Kids—what can you do?*

They walk on. "Why don't we pick up some wine and a video on the way home?" Mitchell says, in hopes of rescuing the remainder of the day.

Kristin falls silent as they head back to Court Street. On the way to the wine shop they pass a toy store called The Funky Monkey. Wincing, Mitchell averts his gaze—to a store window across the street filled with cute little kids' overalls and jumpers. A woman comes out of a Korean deli pushing a double stroller. Twins.

After they buy the wine, which Kristin wouldn't be drinking if she were pregnant, Mitchell is eager to leave the minefield of Court Street and its strollers; he suggests that they walk back along the next street.

"Hey, look," he says, pointing up when they reach the corner of Smith. "They named this one for your alma mater."

Kristin rolls her eyes, but grins.

They walk past a bodega awning topped with multi-colored blinking lights, something out of a Mexican carnival. Next door, a Chinese take-out place has bulletproof Plexiglas above the counter. There are no trees here and the buildings are drab, one or two floors of apartments above meek storefronts. *Arecibo Barber Shop. San Antonio Religious Articles.* A Pakistani sundries shop, all items $1.99 or less. A series of new bistros and sushi restaurants have opened farther down, due to the rising popularity of the neighborhood with young professionals, but this stretch of Smith Street retains a Third World feel. Even the light seems more modest here. Sunbeams illuminate trash along the gutters: an orange scrap of upholstery, a green 7-Up bottle, a white rubber glove. About a mile to the south, the avenue disappears over a hill into a lowering steely cloud.

Mitchell notices a handwritten sign posted on a lamppost that reads *Pit bull 4 sale.* Maybe that wouldn't be such a bad idea, he says to himself, only half joking, thinking of the projects looming around the corner from their new house.

At the next corner he checks out a snow-cone cart topped by a Puerto Rican flag. The sun-leathered old vendor, taking advantage of the last warm days of the year, sits in a folding chair. Two tiny Arab girls step forward, carefully offering up change in their cupped palms, pointing at one of the bottles of syrup, which is filled with a mouthwash-blue liquid. The vendor shakes his head: it seems the girls don't have enough. Mitchell takes out his wallet, raises two fingers, points to the blue liquid. He offers the cones to the little girls. They look up at him warily and exchange a volley of whispers, but after he smiles and nods his head, they accept the gift and skip off around the corner.

A curly-haired bum with a sad clown face staggers by, cursing drunkenly at the world.

Mitchell watches him warily, pondering how far they have come from the Upper East Side.

* * *

At home, they retreat to the backyard to finish reading the paper and savor the last hours of the weekend. Two doors down, the teenage black kid comes out into his yard with a rake. He collects leaves for a few minutes, then goes back inside his house. A moment later he emerges, carrying his boombox.

CHAPTER THREE

GRACE HOWARD

THE NEXT MORNING, GRACE HOWARD RISES JUST AFTER DAWN. SHE holds the neck of her robe shut with one hand as she moves from refrigerator to stove. A lone egg tumbles in a boiling pot.

Outside, the early sun swings shadows of fire escapes over the plaster façades across the court. Grace looks at the salmon-colored house at the end of the row and is reminded of a house brilliant in Caribbean sunshine.

Down in the garden, beads of dew glisten in the light and cherry tomatoes peep out of their green vines. Grace carefully cracks the top of her soft-boiled egg and smiles, eager for her pre-work gardening hour.

After breakfast, she steps into a clean, pressed pair of jeans—a woman in pants; her deacon father would have frowned—and pulls on a sweatshirt sweet with laundry scent. Then she walks down through the basement and out a low shed behind the house. She stands quiet in the doorway so as not to disturb a cardinal poised on the edge of the feeder. Like a machine, the bird processes the sunflower seeds: dips its head, snaps them up in its beak, spits out a spray of shells. Grace coughs; startled, the cardinal springs up and careens off through the trees, leaving black husks of seeds scattered on the walk.

The morning is warm enough that Grace can step out of the doorway barefoot; the wet grass tickles her toes. The garden is so serene at this hour. Lately, Jamel Wilson down the row has taken to playing a radio in his yard, but the boy is never out this early. Across the way, her friend Carol opens her kitchen window and leans her big frame out to wave hello. Carol's mimosa shades the back of the garden. It's a beautiful tree, with its pink graduation cap tassels hanging down, but a dirty one. Grace is always picking up the fern zippers it drops into her yard.

In the yard next door one of the new neighbors, a young white man in a business suit, steps out holding a cup of coffee. He smiles briefly and nods, but makes no conversation. He and his wife have only been here for two months, but Grace won't be surprised if they keep to themselves. Down in the Islands, everybody lived on each other's porches, fanning themselves and talking, but New Yorkers often live in their own private worlds.

Morning glories twine over the fence. Below them, a bed of lobelia radiates electric blue like a school of tiny Islands fish. This is a good place for a garden. The sun doesn't shine year round as it did on Barbados, but the southern exposure helps.

Before Grace moved in, the house had gone long unrented and the backyard was a mess, a sea of weeds and thigh-high grass. After she cleared the yard, it was up to her to design her garden from scratch. For inspiration she took the subway to the Brooklyn Botanic Garden, with its arbors and wandering paths and trellises swarming with roses. The brightest colors, though, were the Sunday dresses of the Islands women from Eastern Parkway, come to promenade under the cherry blossoms with their beaux. Wedding parties posed for photographs, ranks of proud men in tuxedos and women in yards of magenta taffeta, glossy in the sun. Grace walked shyly past, soaking in sweet accents of home. Then she went home to her solitary garden and dug until her muscles ached.

* * *

At work, she stands in the Hamilton Room surveying the evenly spaced luncheon tables, the neat-set silverware. Crystal water goblets brim with the light flooding in through the windows, which offer a spectacular view from forty-seven stories above Manhattan:

the thicket of financial towers downtown, the pewter surface of the Hudson gleaming dully to the west, the souvenir-size Statue of Liberty far to the south. Everything looks perfect for this gathering of the executives and board of one of the world's foremost insurance companies—until Grace notices that all of the floral centerpieces are missing.

She hurries down the hall to Mr. Conway's office, where his secretary Janine sits behind her desk listening intently to her Dictaphone. She's a pretty young redhead, but today she looks tired and stressed.

She glances up as Grace walks in, sees that something is wrong, and takes off her headphones. Before Grace can even say anything, her eyes open wide. "Oh my God, the flowers! Grace, I'm so sorry! My daughter's had a bad flu all week and I haven't gotten any sleep."

"Did you put in the order at all?"

Janine shakes her head, scared now.

Grace looks at her watch: the luncheon will start in just two-and-a-half hours. "Don't worry," she tells Janine calmly, though she knows that Mr. Conway has threatened to fire employees for less. She picks up a phone book. When she reaches their usual florist, she's told that they can't possibly put together twelve complicated centerpieces in time.

Janine looks as if she's about to burst into tears.

Grace pats her on the shoulder. "It's just some silly flowers," she says, picking nervously at a cuticle. She thinks for a moment.

She checks the phone book and writes a couple of numbers on a Post-It. "Call both of these places and ask them how many bouquets they can make by eleven-thirty. Let's keep it simple—just red and orange roses. I'll call the other florists in the neighborhood."

* * *

Two hours later, Grace is still waiting for the deliveries in the doorway of the Hamilton Room. She hears a noise behind her and turns. At the far end of the hall a French door swings open and Ed Laidlaw, the company's chief executive, appears. His stiff-shouldered walk reminds her of Johnny Carson (as does his alert, owlish way of swiveling his bald head above those shoulders, and the way his affability masks a steely will). Back in the Seventies she had started in the typing pool and he—fresh from the Marines—was just a clerk. Over the years she rose to become office manager of this top floor, while he turned into this distinguished man who would look at home in a painting of the founders of the Republic.

He strides toward her over a carpet pale-blue-and-white like the Wedgewood bowls on the Chippendale sideboards. While the other corridors of this executive floor showcase the company's phenomenal collection of American paintings, this muted aisle bears the portraits of the company's CEOs dating back to the late nineteenth century, a row of white men grave with benevolent wisdom.

"How are you today?" Grace asks.

"I'm fine." Her boss glances into the Hamilton Room. Thankfully, he seems distracted this morning.

"Where are you seating our French Victor-India-Papas?" he asks. Mr. Laidlaw uses the military alphabet around the office for a lark: *Tango* for *T*, *Uncle* for *U* . . .

"They'll be to the right of the podium, with Mr. Gibson."

"Excellent. Thanks for the good work, as always."

Grace returns a small guilty smile.

"I'd better make a couple of calls before lunch," he says, but pauses and touches her elbow. "Listen, we've seen a lot of years go under the bridge together, so there's something I wanted to tell you personally. I'm not going to announce this until the new year, so I'd appreciate it if you'd keep it between us for now."

"What is it, Edward?" she asks gently, afraid he has some bad medical news. Over the past several years he has undergone two heart operations.

"I'm going to take early retirement next summer. With my ticker the way it is, I want to relax a little, spend time with my grandkids, play a little golf."

Surprised and moved, Grace puts her hand to her cheek. For so many years he has been her boss, yet also—in his rather stiff, formal way—her friend. "I don't know what to say."

He smiles ruefully. "Just say goodnight, Gracie."

* * *

Half an hour later, as the board members arrive for lunch, Grace stands at the side of the door holding a seating chart. Janine nearly runs down the hall in advance of the guests.

"Don't worry," Grace says quietly, afraid that the secretary will burst out sobbing when she sees that each table now bears a small centerpiece. They're not all identical, but the men won't notice. "I owe you my life," Janine whispers, gripping Grace's arm. Grace smiles. "It was nothing."

The board members straggle down the hall in clumps, two or three gray-suited gentlemen at a time, and murmur polite pleasantries as they enter the room. Mr. Matthews, the only African-American on the board, smiles and walks up to Grace. They chat for a moment about the weather, about a film he saw the previous night. She looks away, concerned that the others will see the only two people of color in the room together and make some stereotypical conclusion.

"I hope you'll be sitting down to eat with us," he says in his courteous North Carolina accent.

"Oh, no, I *couldn't*," she says. "Excuse me, I have to check on something." She glides around him only to be struck, on the other side of the room, by a pang of loneliness. Mr. Matthews is a handsome, distinguished-looking man. And single, too, after a recent divorce. Does he feel the way she does? Though this place has been her home for thirty-five years, in some ways she still feels distanced from these convivial executive faces. In the typing pool, though the work was dull, it had its compensation of sociability; white and black and Latina women working side by side, eating together at lunch. Now she eats alone at her desk or in dry meetings in one of the private dining rooms. And she never invites an executive to dine at her home. What would they make of her Brooklyn neighborhood, these people who live in Larchmont and Greenwich? After all these years she could afford to move out of the city, too, but where, when she got the urge, could she buy plantains or tamarind juice? Where would she promenade on Sundays to hear the voices of her home?

During the luncheon she roams the periphery of the room, preoccupied with making sure that the new corporate dining manager is catering to the executives' special needs: Diet Coke instead of wine for Mr. Gibson, no salad dressing for Mr. Conway.

While the waiters serve coffee; she stands in a corner and watches her boss. His sudden news sinks in. For decades, Ed Laidlaw has been like a tree overshadowing the center of a garden: when he uproots himself, what other shoots may find the light to rise? Mr. Gibson, she feels sure, will be the successor to the executive suite. Mr. Conway or Mr. Perry will step into Gibson's shoes. A couple of times over the past several years she has hinted to Ed Laidlaw that she would be interested in becoming Director of Hospitality Services if the job ever opened up. She doesn't have a background in business, but she has organized many social functions here. She knows that she can never go back to the easy sociability of the typing pool, but maybe if she gets onto the executive track she will no longer be caught between two worlds, will finally be able to relax in her own skin.

She looks up to see Charles Matthews smiling at her from across the room.

* * *

At home at the end of the day, she steps gratefully out of her high heels. (Other women at the office keep a pair of sneakers under their desks to wear home at the end of the day, but she considers this undignified. She doesn't want to be mistaken for a cleaning lady on the subway ride home.) In the bathroom, she swallows a couple of Tylenol, hoping they'll assuage the headache she has felt building throughout the day—so much pressure to make everything perfect. She changes into comfortable clothes and makes a cup of tea, waiting patiently for the water to boil.

Finally, she glides out into the garden, places the teacup on a wrought iron table and settles gratefully into a chair. She closes her eyes for a moment and massages her temples—already she can feel the tension slipping away. She opens her eyes and looks up into the trees, at the heart of this gently waving sea of green, this small world she has made for herself.

Then, as the sky over the rooftops fades, as the air grays in the invisible smoke of dusk, the show begins. Out of the corner of her eye, she catches a sudden flash of yellow. She turns to the evening primrose bush. With a silent Pop! a second yellow blossom opens. Every dusk the primroses bloom, like a tiny fireworks show, like a world of possibilities sparking in the fading light.

CHAPTER FOUR

JAMEL WILSON

JAMEL WILSON WAKES AT TEN, BUT LIES IN BED ANOTHER FIFTEEN minutes until he hears the front door close. He hurries to the window. Down in the street, his mother is fiddling with the gate; she pushes it forward to make sure it's tightly shut. Jamel pulls on some sweatpants and an old Knicks jersey and thumps down to the kitchen, where he sticks a couple of frozen waffles in the toaster.

The waffles aren't quite brown yet, but he pries them out, impatient. It's going to be a long day until his friend Tree comes over and they can walk to the Fulton Street Mall, where his heart's desire is at, waiting for him right now.

Munching on his breakfast, he trots down through the paneled rec room in the basement and out into the back. In the yard next door the leaves of a thin white tree shimmy in the breeze like clusters of green coins. The dog runs up and nuzzles Jamel's leg. He shoves it away and it slinks off into a corner behind the barbecue.

Warmed by the sun, Jamel pulls the jersey over his head and rolls his shoulders, readying himself for work on a special project: a big dead tree in the rear of the yard that crashed down during a summer thunderstorm. He has broken off the branches, but the trunk still lies next to the fence. He spits on his hands and picks up an ax, raises it high overhead and enjoys the solid whunk of blade on log.

An occasional shout of kids at recess wafts over the rooftops from a nearby school, bringing back memories of the grim interior of his high school and making him thankful that last year after eleventh grade he was old enough to drop out. His mother tried to get him to see a guidance counselor, but there was only one for twelve hundred students; it had been so hard to get an appointment that she finally gave up.

The yard is too quiet. He turns back into the basement, jacks up the window, and lifts his boombox onto the sill. Time for some DXZ Crew.

Back in the yard, he swings the ax to the rhythm of the Crew's heavy beats. Soon satisfying rivulets of sweat run down his back. He stops to contemplate the perspiration beading on his skin: like Stephon Marbury stepping off the court at halftime. The music energizes him, even though the little speakers can't muster up enough bass. He stirs his arms from side to side, hips swinging in the opposite direction, as he chants along with the CD: *Gimme da gat!/ Gimme da gat!/ I'm gonna bust a fuckin' cap/ In ya sorry nigga's hat/ Like Chow Yun-Fat takin' it to the mat . . .*

After ten minutes of thwacking away at the wood, he realizes that—except for a small pile of chips he has managed to hack out—the log is undiminished.

Down in the basement, he wipes his chest with the balled-up jersey and pulls a couple sets of bicep curls. He pauses to regard himself in a mirror propped against the wall, pleased by his baseball-sized biceps and by the fact that his goatee is growing in strongly enough this time that he might not have to shave it off before his friends give him grief. He squares his shoulders, trying to make his long torso seem less skinny. He makes a face, lets out his breath, and strides across the cool linoleum floor. Up a short stairway, he pushes aside the iron plates of the storm cellar door in front of the house.

Squinting against the sunlight, he screws a hose into a rusty faucet and adjusts the spraygun for a concentrated blast. He idly hoses down the little concrete yard, spinning leaves and other debris out under the iron railing and into the street. He tries to gun down a yellow jacket in midair but the wasp gets angry and dive-bombs him. He yelps, drops the hose, and flees. Unmanned, the hose writhes in circles, hissing and spraying water every which-a-way. Cursing, Jamel darts back

and wrestles it to a halt. He looks around to see if any neighbors have
seen him.

Two houses down the front door opens and a woman steps out.
One of the new neighbors. Her blonde hair is tied back in a severe
ponytail and she wears a faded sweatshirt that says *Smith*. He looks
on in mild contempt: don't these people have any self-respect? They
wear old sweatpants, gray sneakers, torn shirts. White people don't
know how to dress; either they wear something old and sloppy, or
uptight business clothes with no style, or something wack like the
punk rockers he sometimes sees taking the F train to Manhattan, all
done up in sorry-ass Halloween costumes. Why do these people want
to go running around for no good reason, anyhow?

* * *

Just before noon, Shanice pushes opens the front gate, pausing to shift
the baby to her other hip. Jamel is dismayed to see her friends Brenda
and Lavonne trail through after. He finds it hard enough to talk to the
mother of his child alone—she always starts out with an advantage
on these visits since everyone but his mother has agreed to paint him
as the sole culprit in the matter.

Once, during one of the first times she and her friends brought the
baby over from her apartment in the Wysocki Houses, he made some
small complaint about the burdens of fatherhood. Lavonne stamped
her foot, waved her hands palm out in front of her, and said "What
you know about bein' a favah?! It's her and her moms who take care
of this child. And if you din't want no baby, you shouldn't have done
nothin' to her in the first place," to a chorus of *That's rights* and *You tell
him, girls* from the peanut gallery. And what could he say to that?

Now he doesn't open his mouth; just sits on the stoop gazing off
down the street, trying to keep his cool. He sneaks a look at Shanice
while she fusses with the baby's knit cap. Unlike many young mothers
he's seen, who plump up or lose concern for their appearance, she still
looks good: she has taken a great deal of trouble to do her hair, with
two ringlets hanging down over her ears and a perfect curl lacquered

to her forehead. Even under a flannel shirt and a Polo windbreaker, he can see the fullness of her breasts. But she has consented to sleep with him only once since LaTisha was born, and she made such a big production out of that—as if she was doing him some huge favor—that he's unwilling to be seen out in public as her mate.

"Say hi to your Daddy," she says, holding up the baby, so wrapped up in layers of clothes that her arms and legs jut out stiffly, as if she was a miniature Thanksgiving Parade float. Wide-eyed, Tisha grimaces and pushes against her mother's shoulder with a tiny plump hand.

Shanice sets her down. The baby stands unsteady, rocking back and forth, and then walks straight toward the basement stairs.

"Don't put her down here," Jamel says. "One day she gonna fall right down them steps."

Shanice scoops the baby up. "Why don't *you* hold her then?"

Her friends look on in amusement as she hands the baby over. Jamel takes hold of his daughter gingerly, afraid of dropping her, worried that her diaper may need a change. He cups his palm behind Tisha's little head, over her wispy whorly hair, and looks down, awed as always by the little rumbling beanbag pressed against his chest.

* * *

Finally, around two o'clock, after the girls have gone, up the street comes Tree, ambling along on his stilt legs. Jamel's best friend's real name is Terrence, but ever since he had a growth spurt in Seventh Grade, the nickname has stuck. Onica, half his size, walks along beside him, hands tucked into her red down jacket. A funny-looking couple, but inseparable.

"Yo, hurry up," Jamel says.

Tree's long face breaks open in his sweet, goofy smile. "Take it light," he says. Tree's parents died when he was a little boy. Though officially his aunt is his guardian—and they have a unit in the Wysocki projects—he has practically lived at Jamel's ever since.

"We going to B.P.W.?" asks Onica, referring to Black People's World, Tree's name for the Fulton Street Mall. She reaches up and adjusts a clip in her curly orange hair. Her skin has an orange cast too, and her face is peppered with freckles.

"We going," Jamel says. "Let me change real quick." Upstairs, he slides into some baggy new FUBU jeans, a Tommy Hilfiger jersey, a Knicks watch cap, and his spotless Air Jordans. Then he and his friends set off, around the corner and past the giant brick Wysocki Houses.

"Don't even look at 'em," says Tree in a mocking high voice.

"Yo, fuck you, man." Jamel scowls, not at all amused by this impression of his mother, who has threatened that if he doesn't stay away from the projects, he'll be sent to live with an aunt down South. Make one mistake, he has to pay for it his whole life.

With the way all hell broke out afterward, it's hard to remember the glory of the party that night. The dark apartment, the music loud and grinding, young bodies crammed into a room, a sweet smell of perfume and sweat. He took Shanice by the hand and led the way back to her bedroom. Lying on her bed, under her girlish innocent posters of TLC and Brandy and Mary J. Blige, he kissed her eager plum lips, felt the pulsing of her firm breasts under his hand. And then he slid his hand up her quivering thigh, and slipped a finger under the silk of her panties, into another silk, and he was shocked by the wonder of it, warm and soft and fleshy and slick as pearl and faintly grainy deep within and wet. *I'm a man*, he thought. *A man*.

"Yo, Erf to Spock," says Tree, and Jamel snaps out of his reverie. A block away from the Wysocki Houses the side streets fancy up dramatically, rows of renovated brownstones and old brick houses carefully maintained. Jamel's mother sells properties for a local real estate office. She comes home disgusted these days, talking about how most of the white buyers who are invading the neighborhood seem to be taking their money to the white-owned agencies up on Court Street.

On the day the new couple moved in, Mr. and Mrs. Jogger, Jamel sat on his front stoop, watching the moving men unload all sorts of furniture, brand-new and expensive-looking. His mother sat next to him, looking like she'd just bitten into something sour.

"What's 'a matter?" he said.

"Used to be, a black family wanted to work hard and move up a little, they could buy a house 'round here. Them people"—she nodded toward the neighbors—"thought this area was too run-down. They stayed up in the Slope or the Heights. But then they figured they like the old houses, fix 'em up, and now they can't leave us alone. You got people paying more than a million for some busted-up place." She snorted. "Only reason they ain't drove us all out is the projects: scares most of 'em too much, the idea of living 'round the corner from thousands of poor black folk."

* * *

Across Atlantic Avenue, though, as Jamel and his friends approach the mall, almost every passing face is black or Pakistani or Latino. Storekeepers, bus drivers, security guards, even the cops. Nobody crosses nervously to the other side of the street when he walks along; nobody pretends not to hear when he orders a slice of pizza. He can go into Macy's without being followed around every second by suspicious security guards. Black People's World.

Even blocks away he can feel the energy of the mall. First there's the music in the air, a patchwork of sound shifting as he walks, the smooth Seventies arrangements behind Al Green overlapped by the slinky bass lope of Snoop Dogg, surrendering to the fast growly chant of a Jamaican dance hall CD. A boombox propped on a glove vendor's stand delivers a distorted reggae beat and the lyric "Santa was a black man." And then there are the smells: West Indian roti and beef patties, fried chicken and shrimp, sweet perfume wafting up from bundles of incense on a card table laid out with books promoting African culture.

"Yo, J, slow up," complains Onica, but he strides on toward Fulton Street, passing beneath second-story signs for driver-training schools, bail bondsmen, personal injury lawyers. The sounds build to a pitch as he walks out onto the open mall. A bus stops to pick up passengers, doors opening with a mechanical pull-tab hiss. A one-legged woman in a wheelchair jingles a change cup. "Five dollars!" shouts a sidewalk salesman next to a shopping bag spilling out boxer shorts. "I got Calvin! I got Polo! Five dollars! Five!"

Jamel pauses, stepping out of the river of shoppers thronging the sidewalks to lean against a wall and pry a pink wad of gum off the bottom of his shoe. Next to his hand, a poster reads "DL Promotions presents Earth Ruler King Sound! Special Guest Appearances by Turbo Belly and Nitty Kutchie, featuring, from Spanish Town Jamaica, Killa Manjaro! XXTra tight security. Doors open 10 p.m. at Aristocrat Manor on Empire Boulevard." The show sounds wild but he shakes his head; it's just another place his mother wouldn't let him go.

On the corners stand clumps of homeboys from the projects, wearing do-rags, baggy jeans drooping over the tops of their unlaced Timberlands. Jamel watches them out of the corner of his eye, envious of their aura of cool menace. They don't just listen to the music—they live it. One of them's a short but dangerous kid who goes by the name Tee-Ali; he has a dent on one side of his head and always wears narrow wraparound sunglasses. He recognizes Jamel, walks over, and grabs him in a headlock.

"Whussup, PeeWee?" he says, pulling off Jamel's Knicks cap and burning his knuckles into his hair.

Jamel is unhappy that the homeboys from the projects still tag him with this nickname, despite the fact that he's grown a good eight inches in the last couple of years. In fact, he's now taller than Tee-Ali, although it would be unwise to point this out—even in the rough-and-tumble world of the projects, Tee-Ali has a reputation. It's said that he robbed a Housing Authority inspector in the stairwell of Building Three and was involved in the beating of a jogger in Prospect Park.

"Get offa me," Jamel says, hating the whine in his voice.

Tee-Ali's affable expression ices over. "Say what, bitch?"

"I ain't say nothin'," Jamel mumbles. He looks around for Tree and Onica, but they're engrossed in a store window halfway down the block. His knees feel weak as Tee-Ali stares at him for a moment through his impenetrable shades.

"Yo, Pee-Wee, lend me a dollar."

A couple of Tee-Ali's friends wander over to watch.

"I din't bring no money."

"Is that right?" Tee-Ali reaches around behind Jamel and tugs his wallet out of his back pocket. "You gonna have to give up *five*, now," he says. He pulls out a bill and thrusts the wallet into Jamel's chest.

Tee-Ali's friends snicker. Jamel feels the blood rush to his face.

"You wanna say somethin'?"

Almost imperceptibly, Jamel shakes his head.

Tee-Ali shoves him away—"Hasta la vista, *ponk*"—and struts off with his crew.

Tree and Onica turn back to find Jamel.

"Yo, what happen?" Onica asks.

"Nothin'," Jamel says. Rigid with frustration and rage, he stares at Tee-Ali and his friends laughing on their corner. *If I had a Mac-9*, he thinks, *muthafucka be dead right now*. A hot tear forces its way into the corner of his eye. He knows he's not going to get a gun, and even if he did, it would be suicide to go up against Tee-Ali's crew.

Fired again with his initial sense of purpose, he hurries on. The avenue's a collage of plastic signs, bright block colors, green, black, red, yellow, neon, glitter, shouting *We Buy Gold! All Items $10 or Less! Everything Must Go!* It's a great bazaar where shoppers can buy everything from beepers to cheap bedsheets to bootlegs of movies that haven't even hit the theaters. Jamel ignores the lure of the countless sales pitches, threading through the crowd like a fish swimming upstream, moving forcefully toward his true destination.

Onica stops outside a tiny Pakistani street stall. She picks up a scarf and looks at Tree, who shrugs.

"Come *on*," Jamel says, pulling at her sleeve. He leads his friends through the door of Premier Electronics, sighs: *At last*.

"Can I help you?" says the Chinese man behind the counter.

"Naw, I know what I want," Jamel replies. He steps past rows of toaster ovens and microwaves and clock radios gleaming under the fluorescent lights, heads straight for the cork-padded sound room in the back, where he finally stops before a set of four mighty speaker cabinets covered in rugged gray felt and faced with a wire grill. He

brushes his hand respectfully over the SuperDJ 400-watt power amplifier and the sloping multi-channel mixer. He looks up at his friends
with a proud grin, imagining the day when he'll set up this system in
his basement. He'll rule the block, with a barbecue in the backyard
every afternoon, a party in the basement every night, soundtrack
courtesy of Jay-Z, Biggie Smalls, and DXZ Crew. He imagines turning the bass up so loud they'll even hear him over in the projects.
Tee-Ali will have to show some respect if he wants to be allowed in.
Gimme da gat!

"Check it out," he says. "This gonna be mine's."

"How you gonna afford that shit?" Tree asks, though they both
know the answer: Jamel's mother will do just about anything to keep
her son happy at home, away from the Wysocki Houses.

CHAPTER FIVE

"Hey, Milo, ain't your wife been feedin' you?"

Milosz, cutting a piece of veal parmigiana, looks up sharply at Carol's uncle Dominic. "What do you mean?"

"You're eatin' like it's goin' outta style."

Milosz's eyes narrow in suspicion at this unfamiliar idiom. "My wife cooks for me all the time."

"He's just kidding, honey," Carol says, laying her hand on her husband's shoulder. "Don't pay any attention. And you"—she turns to her uncle—"How many times do I have to tell you? It's *Mee-lowsh.*"

"All right," says Dominic, raising his hands in mock surrender. "I'll get it right one of these times."

Milosz rises and Carol watches him make his way across the dance floor toward the buffet. Though slight in build, he walks with a sailor's tight-necked swagger. *Like Popeye*, she thinks fondly. What she had originally seen as shyness seems to have been a result of the language barrier and his unfamiliarity with American ways; as his English improves, a cockiness emerges.

"He's kind of tetchy," says Uncle Dominic.

"It's hard for him, not knowing anybody," Carol replies. "Be nice."

A clinking of glasses sweeps the hall, a vaulted Bay Ridge ballroom decorated with Italianate frescoes. At the head table, the groom leans over to kiss the bride. *What a mistake*, Carol thinks to herself for the tenth time this day. The bride is pretty, but very modest and polite, while so far the groom has impressed Carol as a loudmouth and a boor.

She's not alone in her opinion. During a visit to the ladies' room, she emerges from a stall to find her friend Stacy Martella rearranging the shoulder pads of her fuchsia satin dress.

"This place is over the top," Carol says. "Did you see the signs outside the bathroom doors: 'Mermaids' and 'Mermen'?"

"Don't knock it," Stacy replies. "If you knew what this reception was costing, you'd die. Wow, look at these little soaps—like perfect seashells."

"If I stay in here too long, I'm gonna have to pee again," Carol says, nodding toward the corner of the bathroom, where a little waterfall trickles into what looks like a Jacuzzi tiled with clamshells.

"Don't make me laugh," says Stacy, trying to separate some clumped-together eyelashes.

"What's with these waiters? They shouldn't put their tuxes in the dryer—the poor old guys look like a bunch of chimps."

Stacy sputters with laughter. "Don't start, Fasone. I'll ruin my makeup. So, whaddaya you think of the groom?"

"I'm not sure about this guy."

"Are you kidding? Let me tell you—last night when we're leaving the rehearsal dinner, he tells her he doesn't think her shoes go with her dress. Which they do—she bought everything at Kleinfeld, and it looks gorgeous—but he just wants to give her a hard time. Next thing you know, they're out on the sidewalk shoutin' to wake the dead, and he puts his fist through the glass panel in the door of O'Reilly's."

"It's tough."

As they exit, they both tuck a soap into their purses. Back in the reception hall they skirt the dance floor, where the bride and groom are clasped together in their first dance, "Wind Beneath My Wings." Carol sits and watches, tears rising to her eyes despite the picture's hidden flaws.

Milosz returns, bearing another helping of cannelloni and veal. She's pleased to see him eating so heartily; usually he pushes his dinner away with food still on the plate. "Do you remember our first dance?" she asks.

He nods shortly and turns his full attention to his food, first sawing the meat into neat bite-size pieces and then conveying them to his mouth one after another, jaw muscles bunching as he eats.

The first time she took him to an American supermarket, he kept turning around, picking up items and turning them over in bewilderment. "What is this *Shake 'n Bake?*" "What is this *Pop Tarts?*" He pointed in confusion at a long aisle of cereal boxes. "All this is for breakfast?" He picked up a box. "What is this *Count Chocula?*" Carol offered to learn how to make some Bosnian recipes, thinking that he might be homesick, but he wanted only American food. She worked hard to feed him, yet he gained barely a couple of pounds.

He drops his napkin on the table, leans back, and rolls a cigarette. In the background, Sinatra sings.

"Will you dance with me?" Carol asks.

He lights his smoke. "Maybe later."

Fairy tales/ Can come true—

"Please, honey."

Milosz takes a deep drag of his cigarette. He shrugs, then smiles a sheepish smile that makes her melt. He stands, undoes his bowtie, and lets it hang around his neck. He looks so handsome in his rented tuxedo. His face betrays no effort as he guides her out across the floor. She's glad she thought to wear flats. (In her own wedding video, Milosz looked several inches shorter because she wore heels.) Normally, in her size 14 clothes, she thinks of herself as big and awkward, but now—as her husband glides her around the room—she feels like Ginger Rogers. She looks around the swirling hall, beaming with pride, as if to say *Look at me now, look at the Carol Fasone who used to stay home every Friday night eating whole pints of ice cream, watching TV, driven nearly out of her mind by her mother's incessant comments.*

The DJ puts on a Gloria Estefan record and Milosz coolly switches gears, foxtrot to merengue.

"How did you learn to dance so well in the middle of all that fighting?" she asks, imagining him in some shell-ravaged Bosnian ballroom.

He sweeps her back into a dip. "The war was not all of life."

* * *

After the reception, Milosz helps the groom load the wedding gifts into the trunk of a waiting limo. Carol stands on the sidewalk, glad of the warm wrap she's thrown over her bare shoulders. In the distance, near the end of Fourth Avenue, a tower of the Verrazano Bridge rises above some apartment buildings, lit up like a giant green tuning fork.

A valet brings their car around. Carol reaches into her pocketbook and gives Milosz a couple of dollars. She nudges him.

"What?"

"Give it to the guy," she whispers.

"Why?"

"It's a tip."

He frowns, dubious about this American extravagance. He pulls out onto the avenue.

"Wasn't that a nice party?" Carol asks, pulling the seat belt across her chest.

"The food was good."

"I'm a little worried about her husband, though. Didn't he seem kind of rough for her?"

Milosz shrugs. "Simmed like an okay guy to me."

She turns and looks out the window at dark Fourth Avenue. Soon hulking apartment buildings and churches give way to a strip of auto collision shops and fix-a-flat garages. She sinks back against the headrest and sighs, full of good food, buzzed on sugar and champagne. She remembers sitting in the pew of the church, looking back to watch the bride proceed up the aisle. Even the jerk of a groom seemed choked up at how beautiful she looked, sweeping slowly forward under her veil. And Carol's disappointment in him was temporarily set aside by the magic of the ceremony, that bright shining bubble floating above life's flat reality. *Do you take this woman. . . ? Till death do you part.* She had asked Milosz for his handkerchief. He sat back dry-eyed, gazing blankly into space. Men were so boring sometimes, so devoid of imagination.

She turns now to his impassive profile. Occasionally a passing streetlamp lights up a cowlick in the back of his short-cropped hair. He talks so little that she rarely knows what he's thinking. Well, in a few minutes they'll be home, and then—once they get into bed— maybe she can reach him in a different way. Maybe tonight he'll stop her before she takes her diaphragm from the bedside drawer. "Put that away," he'll say. "We don't need that anymore."

During a lunch break recently she walked over to the library and pored over a book of baby names. That night after dinner, when she handed Milosz the list she had compiled, he picked up a dictionary off his desk, flippantly calling out words at random. "If it's a boy, we can name him *Laminate*. If a girl, *Isopod*." She laughed along, smiling stupidly to mask the sting.

They pull to a stop before a red light. Across the avenue, a car burns rubber coming out of a McDonald's parking lot. She waits until the light changes before she speaks, figuring that it might be easier to broach the subject again if he's occupied with driving.

"Don't you ever think about what it would be like to have a son?" she asks, appealing to his sense of macho.

"How can we bring children into such a world?" he asks gravely. The witness to untold suffering—after sarcasm, this is his second tack when he wants to avoid the issue. A bicyclist weaves through the traffic ahead, the red safety light strapped to his ankle spinning in dizzy circles. "That was good champagne," Milosz says calmly, as if the question of children is resolved. And, a minute later, "Remind me to set the alarm for early when we get home; I must to meet with my faculty advisor tomorrow morning."

Carol looks out the side window, pressing her tongue against the inside of her cheek. All the women's magazines say communication is the essential ingredient of a good relationship, that she must make it clear that her needs are as important as her spouse's. But if she presses too hard, won't she run the risk of spoiling what they have, of driving him away? She grips the seat belt, pulling it tight across her chest.

Milosz stretches his arm across the seat and strokes the back of her neck. After a moment, she relaxes back into the seat. She turns her head and kisses his palm, thinking only about how they'll share the rest of the evening.

* * *

She rises in the middle of the night, walking stilted and tentative in the dark she has preserved so as not to wake her husband. In the bathroom at the rear of the apartment, a sharp rectangle of light lies coldly on the tiles. She gazes out the window at a moon so bright it's hard to believe its light is only reflected.

With a click of the light switch, the moonbeam disappears. After she pees, Carol stands at the sink, enjoying the rush of water over her half-sleeping hands, remembering the lovemaking earlier in the night. She glances down at the tile floor where a faint sticky spot in front of the toilet catches the light. Even with his pee-stains around the porcelain, his dirty coffee cups abandoned throughout the apartment like interrupted thoughts, it's good to have a man in the house. She reaches into the cupboard under the sink, pulls out a spray cleaner, wipes the floor with a wisp of toilet paper.

When she clicks off the light, the room evaporates, bringing back the moon. She pushes aside the musty drapes and raises the window. Out in the garden the rosebushes cast their ghostly shadows across the lawn. The white Madonna beams. Even in the stark moonlight, a muted impression of green remains. A chill breeze scrapes the leaves and Carol shivers—whether from the cold or the faint trace of the supernatural in the air, she cannot say.

Quickly, back down the hall, into the bedroom. She slips under the covers and scoots over against her husband's warm bare back. Milosz's ribs arc under her hand. Maybe they shouldn't watch TV at dinnertime. Even years later, images from Bosnia are still liable to flash across the screen: the sharp recoil and puff of smoke from the barrel of a tank, or decaying bodies being pulled from a mass grave. No wonder he doesn't eat. It even affects their sex life. She presses her face to his neck and inhales his warm scent.

CHAPTER SIX

A s Mitchell rounds the corner, his block is dark; the asphalt shines under the streetlamps as if the source of light were buried down below. He shifts his briefcase to the other hand and slows, remembering his prep school hockey rink in that lonely moment before he'd step out onto the ice. Caught up in the imagined *hiss* and *snick* of sharpened skates, he hears too late the real feet padding up behind.

Turning, he sees a young black guy, but the youth shoves him roughly back around. A second stranger darts out from between two parked cars.

And then he's staring at a knife held six inches in front of his face. His assailants stand behind him; one pins Mitchell's arms back as the other holds up the strange curved blade. It's a linoleum cutter—he used one when he and Kristin laid down their new kitchen floor, a knife so sharp it sliced easily through tiles—

"Don't say nothin'," breathes a voice into his ear.

Panic ices his chest but he's surprised by his lucidity. *I'm being mugged*, he thinks. *This is what it's like to be mugged.* The moment expands with underwater slowness. Don't get stabbed, he tells himself. Just give them the money. "Look," he says, "I'm just going to give you the money."

"You got *that* right," says a voice behind him. The other laughs sharply. "Come with us," the first voice says. He feels himself being pulled from the center of the street toward a murky doorway.

"No," he says, and then—before they get angry—"My wallet's in the front, my right front pocket, okay?"

A hand reaches in, tugs out his wallet. He's slammed back against the hood of a car and then . . . they let him go. He sneaks a look as they brush past and receives several quick impressions: two young black faces, a red-and-blue windbreaker, a baseball cap worn backward. One of them sports that odd look the ghetto kids are into, the waistband of his underwear hitched high above his drooping jeans. To Mitchell's irritation, they slouch off down the street—shouldn't they at least be *running* now?

He waits until they disappear, then jogs homeward, heart thumping, along this corridor roofed with dry November leaves. A few yards away, he comes upon his empty wallet lying on a stretch of asphalt glittering with mica stars. Then he passes a burly, tattooed young man with a tuft of beard under his lip, sitting on a stoop next to a bottle of Heineken, watching him. Watching him get mugged, evidently.

"Gotta look out, guy," the man drawls in a Spanish accent. "Gotta be careful."

"Thanks," Mitchell mutters. "Thanks a lot."

He climbs his own stoop. I shouldn't tell Kristin, he thinks. She'll just worry every time I come home late. But the moment he walks in, his wife realizes something's wrong. She gasps when he tells her what happened; she steps forward and hugs him, and he feels that—despite the rocky times they sometimes have together—they *are* together, and he feels a rush of love.

While she paces the kitchen, eyes wide, he calls the police. Then he waits slumped at the kitchen table, staring down at his blue tie, at the gray pinstriped suit he bought because the padded shoulders make him look more athletic, more capable.

"We haven't even been here four months yet," his wife says. "Maybe this is why the house was so cheap. I knew we shouldn't have trusted that realtor. 'Lively area,' he said. 'An up-and-coming block' . . ."

Mitchell shivers now that the adrenalin has worn off. He shares his wife's bitterness about the agent's sales pitch. "A neighborhood of wonderful Greek Revival and Italianate row houses from the late 1800s, just a stone's throw away from Brooklyn Heights . . ." Which is where they'd be right now if he could afford it, their first home together in a safe enclave of elegant brownstones, instead of this fringe neighborhood of rehabbed brick row houses where you can get mugged out in the street while people sit and watch.

"Honey, maybe we should think about moving," Kristin says.

"Look, this could have happened anywhere in Manhattan," he answers, rationalizing the situation as much for his own benefit as hers. Maybe the best thing would be to pack up immediately and get out, but how can he do that when he's still paying for the closing and the move and the down payment and the rest? "It was just bad luck," he says. "And I didn't get hurt. It was only a couple of kids out to grab a few bucks."

He looks up at his wife's stricken face. Without makeup, under this harsh fluorescent light, she looks thin-lipped and wan. Usually she strikes him as naturally confident, like the NCAA swimmer that she was, but now she seems somehow smaller, frail.

"We'll be fine," he says, as if taking charge. "You're going to take a taxi home anytime after dark, but we'll be fine."

A radio squawks outside and a red light flashes on the front shade. Kristin comes out and stands on the stoop, arms crossed and hugging her sides, while Mitchell descends into the street to talk to two policemen in a squad car. The cop in the passenger seat rolls down the window; he's a big-necked Irish kid whose biceps stretch the short sleeves of his uniform.

"New in the neighborhood, huh?" He gives Mitchell a look that makes him feel foolish. "Listen, I hate to break it to ya, but ya can't just figure by all the nice fixed-up houses on this street—around the corner there ya got some projects, the Wysocki Houses. Colored kids come outta there at night, they grab a wallet or a purse, they run back in. Ya gotta be alert when you're comin' outta the subway, 'cause they're hanging around the corner looking for somebody who isn't paying attention. My advice to you, just in case: transfer most a ya money to an inside pocket and keep a bunch a ones in the wallet.

That way, if ya get robbed ya don't lose much a your paycheck and
they're not gonna be pissed off, 'cause they'll think they grabbed a
wad of cash. It's 'mugger money,' right? Listen, take this"—the cop
hands him a card—"and if ya see the perps out on the street, call the
precinct house and ask for a detective named Schimek. Give him this
case number I wrote down at the bottom, okay?"

"Perps?"

"The *perp*etratuhs—ya know, the kids who robbed ya. Take care
now."

Mitchell stands on the sidewalk and watches the squad car strobe
off down the street. *Perps. Mugger money.* Christ.

Later, he and Kristin make love in a deep, powerful way. *This* is
why I got married, he thinks, gripping her in his arms and burying
his face in her fine, silky hair: this closeness, this merciful bond.

Later still, after she turns the light out, he lies awake, shaken by a
vision of what *could* have happened—a puddle of blood coagulating
under the streetlight . . .

* * *

The next morning at work he leans over the carpeted wall of his cubicle and calls Doug Parken away from his computer. His colleague
loves dress-down Fridays; today he wears green chinos and a faded
chamois shirt. Parken's a big hunting and fishing enthusiast. He's a
quiet guy and Mitchell appreciates that—when he first started working here he had a neighbor who used to whistle and it nearly drove
him crazy.

"You wouldn't believe what happened to me last night," Mitchell
begins.

"Did you struggle or anything?" Parken asks when he gets to the
point where the kids tried to pull him away from the streetlight.

Troubled by his own passive role in the encounter, Mitchell plays
up the forcefulness of the muggers, the size of the knife.

"It would have been a lot different if you'd been carrying," Parken
says.

"Carrying?"

"You know—if you had a gun. Knife versus gun—no contest, am I right?"

"I guess so," Mitchell says, dubious.

* * *

By midday, word has spread around the office and secretaries stop in the hallway to touch him on the shoulder and cluck in sympathy. Each one has her own story to tell: a friend robbed at gunpoint by a hyper crackhead, an aunt shoved down a flight of subway stairs. A certain zeal fires the telling, a relish in the gruesomeness of the details: *It's a jungle out there, but we have survived.*

In the afternoon, as the traders file into the boardroom before the weekly goals meeting, they all ask Mitchell "How much did they get?"—which doesn't strike him as the proper first concern.

At thirty-five he often feels old here, too slow to compete with these husky boys in their mid-twenties, weaned on video games and MTV. Before the boss arrives to start the meeting, they cluster around the huge marble table and compare notes on golf courses in Edinburgh and bars in Tokyo and other places they seem too young to know. Most of them were funneled here directly from the boss's alma mater, the University of Virginia. They live off beer, Chinese food, and the sodas and candy bars provided free in the office kitchen, yet they maintain wrestlers' physiques in the company's fully equipped gym. Mr. Reincke, a.k.a. the Big Man, has indulged their competitive spirit and his own love of deep-sea fishing by organizing the traders into teams: Swordfish, Dolphins, Tarpon, and Marlins. (Barracuda and Sharks, evidently, would have seemed a bit over the top).

Mitchell has always been good with numbers, but the aggressive magic that causes the figures to propagate eludes him. While the traders huddle around their raised semi-circle of desks—talking urgently into headsets like air-traffic controllers; pacing in front of a wall of clocks showing London time, Tokyo time, Sydney time—he sits in a calm corridor, tallying the firm's profits. Some of the accountants jokingly refer to themselves as members of the Flounder team. Most seem happy enough here, like Parken, who is perfectly content to crunch his numbers and collect his paychecks and drive home to his wife and kids near Bucks County every night.

Mitchell feels the tug of a greater ambition. Not to be one of the traders, but to do something more worthwhile with his life. He looks around during the morning commute on the F train, or lies in bed after his wife goes to sleep, and thinks, *You've lived thirty-five of your precious years already; if you were to die now—if you had been stabbed by those muggers—what would you have accomplished? Would you have done anything that helped anybody but yourself?* Sometimes he stares at a spreadsheet and it seems ridiculous—how can grown people spend their lives like this, playing games with money, and think that it means anything? He gets wild urges to drop his job and start a new career. He can't see himself turning to social work, exactly, but he's got a secret dream: he'd love to study at the Culinary Institute up there along the Hudson, then open a restaurant—he could spend his life making people happy by giving them good food, rather than devoting it to this weird speculative business where nobody actually makes anything. He knows he needs to make a change, but he's decided to hang on for another year or two, save some money first.

He moves to the sideboard to pour himself a cup of coffee, then gazes out the huge picture window. This high up, it's clear that Manhattan is indeed an island. Sometimes, working late, he'll take a break to come and sit here in the dark and eat his delivered pizza or spare ribs, soothed by the whisper of the air conditioning within, the shimmering meadows of lights without. Due to changes in weather and light, the view is never the same. He has seen lightning slash down on the Empire State Building; seen near-tropical sunsets blazing above New Jersey's oil refineries; and sometimes—due to whirling blizzards—hardly seen out at all.

Today, the view is clear. Before Mr. Reincke arrives to deliver his locker-room pep talk, Mitchell falls into a familiar daydream: he looks down into the heart of midtown as if into a vast stone quarry and imagines launching himself out in slow motion, swimming between buildings and water towers, drunk with the joy of flying. But then his reverie shifts tone and he sees a landscape of deep canyons and high crags, imagines scores of tiny gray-suited men swan-diving off the ledges. His father avoided such a rapid way out of his financial troubles—and escaped prison—but only after allowing himself (and his family) to suffer two years of financial disembowelments and public humiliations. Even now, sometimes new traders arrive at the office and joke about Mitchell's last name, unaware that he *is*, in fact, the son of Thomas Brett, pioneer of the insider-trading dive.

"Heard about your adventure last night. How much did they get?"

Mitchell looks up to see Mr. Reincke himself. "Not much," he replies, his annoyance with the question mitigated by the glow of the Big Man's attention.

* * *

For another week he compulsively repeats the story of the mugging— to friends, to relatives, to relative strangers. When he gets dressed in the morning, he avoids picking out the same shirt he wore on the night he was mugged. Evenings, he scurries out of the subway and jogs down his block, looking over his shoulder as his briefcase slaps the side of his thigh. Although he reminds himself that the incident had been relatively nonviolent, the sight of a black man coming down the block is enough to make him freeze. The street—the same street he walked down a week ago enjoying the soothing autumn nights—has turned into a charged gauntlet, a danger zone he must pass through to reach the safety of his home.

One afternoon, Detective Schimek calls to ask if he'll stop by the precinct house to look at some mug shots. Fired by a sense of civic responsibility and a greater desire for revenge, Mitchell consents.

After work, he gets off two subway stops earlier than usual. Horns blare from a broad intersection swollen with cars crawling toward the Manhattan Bridge. Trucks whine into lower gear as they mount a ramp to the elevated Brooklyn-Queens Expressway whizzing by to the north, past the burnt-brick towers of another housing project. Mitchell looks on like a lost explorer; how far from the delicate Upper East Side, this scorched landscape of asphalt and metal glaring in the late-day sun.

He enters a side street crammed with diagonally parked squad cars. A couple of cocky off-duty cops push through the door of the station house, wearing baseball jackets, carrying gym bags. Inside, behind the battlement of the cigarette-scarred front desk, a couple of mustached young officers sit deep in a bullpen conversation, in no hurry to deal with whatever his problem may turn out to be. A pretty Hispanic sergeant with bright red lips wanders over, eyebrows raised. Flustered by her mixture of sexiness and authority, Mitchell stammers out Schimek's name. She gives him a room number, waves him past a wooden barrier, points him toward the stairs. With a surge of excitement at being let loose in this regular-guy clubhouse, Mitchell walks unescorted up the green stairwell and then along a drab hallway. Uniformed cops walk by, not with the frenetic urgency of TV cops, but the heavy tread of shift workers with an eye on the clock.

In Room 217 he finds a large office crowded with dented gray desks and filing cabinets, a grubby area that many people use but no one owns. Diffident, he asks for Detective Schimek. Across the room, a beefy middle-aged man calls him over.

"I'm Schimek," the detective says. "Thanks for comin' down." He reaches out a thick, stubby hand; Mitchell notices a holster strapped under his brown polyester sport coat. "Have a seat. Want some coffee?"

Mitchell shakes his head. The detective lifts two big binders out of a cabinet and thumps them down on the desk. "I want you to take your time and look over these pictures. If you see anybody that looks like they might be our boys, even if you're not sure, just call me over. Even if you just get a weird feeling about a picture . . ."

Mitchell certainly does get a weird feeling as he opens the over-stuffed binder to find rows of Polaroids fitted into plastic sleeves. Every face is black. Black or dark brown, light brown, even a couple of albinos. The men and boys in the pictures, freshly arrested, are a scarred, sullen gallery. They stand awkwardly, in profile and then facing the bright flash head-on, and he's chilled by their blankness, their dull lack of response.

He leafs through the second binder. He doesn't want to disappoint Schimek, this confident man who's on his side, but none of the faces calls up even a glimmer of recognition. The detective takes this news with a stolid shrug.

"Are these pictures from all over the city?" Mitchell asks.

Schimek chuckles. "No, sir, all these gentlemen are our friends from the Wysocki Houses. Thank you. We'll call if anything else comes up."

* * *

On the way home, Mitchell almost trips over a baby carriage on the sidewalk and realizes he's been lost in a fantasy of meeting the muggers on his street again. In actuality he just stood there, letting them take his money without a murmur of protest, but he makes up for it in his daydreams. The youths bump into him and laugh—until he pulls out a gun. He makes them lie down on the sidewalk and orders them to pray.

CHAPTER SEVEN

WHEN SHE RETURNS FROM THE CAFETERIA WITH A CUP OF COFFEE, Grace notices that the red light is blinking on her office phone. She removes the plastic top of the cup, sits down, and retrieves her messages. This late in the day it's probably some anxious executive, calling to say that he forgot to request a conference room for a Monday meeting. Or maybe Mr. Gibson, wanting to know if she has found him a new secretary yet.

But the voice emerging from the receiver is at once strange and familiar. As she sips her drink she hears a throat-clearing cough, then a deep, resonant, "Hello, this is Charles Matthews, calling at . . . uh, just before five o'clock. I'm sorry to trouble you at work, but I . . . actually I'm not calling in regard to the Beardon Group. That is"—another cough—"I was wondering if you would care to have dinner with me sometime next week. I hope this doesn't seem too out of the blue. I can be reached at"—and he proceeds to give his numbers at home and at his office, which, if Grace remembers correctly from her board list, is down near Wall Street.

She repeats the message—perhaps she misinterpreted it. No, there it is again: "care to have dinner."

She pushes her fingertips against her mouth and gazes absently about her office. A date. He's calling to ask for a *date*. A little puff of a laugh escapes her, but her heart clenches. Discovering the coffee cup in her hands, she sets it carefully on her desk.

He'll be expecting a reply. Panicked, she glances at the clock. It's well after five now. She decides to pretend that she left work before receiving the message—that will buy her the weekend before she's forced to decide what to do.

* * *

After work, she stops into a deli for some ice cream, provisioning herself for a comfortable evening with *Frontline* and then a historical romance. (She believes she should be reading more intellectually stimulating books, but she's usually too tired. Besides, the guilt intensifies the pleasure.)

At home, she sets her groceries down and turns the radio on for some company, hoping that New York's West Indian station won't be playing the aggressive dance hall reggae which seems to be taking over these days. She waters the poinsettia and the African violet in the kitchen. She sets the watering can on the table. She looks down to discover a circle of water spreading from the bottom of the can onto some work papers. She mops up the wet, then drifts down the hall to the bathroom, where she absently stares into the mirror. She places a hand over her collar. "He must be crazy," she murmurs. Look at this middle-aged woman: this sagging neck, this too-broad face, these dark-circled eyes.

And then, as often happens, she gets the strange sensation that the woman in the mirror with the crow's feet and graying hair—this woman is not really her. When she asks herself how old she really feels, the answer comes back: inside, she is still a nineteen-year-old arriving in a new country, dragging a huge suitcase, heart filled with fear and hope. Or, at most, thirty-one, the age her mother was when she died, the age her mother will always be.

A postcard over the laundry hamper catches her eye, a Winslow Homer watercolor of a small boat adrift on a boundless sea. *This is what Charles Matthews is asking*, she thinks. *He wants me to push off from everything I know into a preposterous adventure. A date. It's been years. Perhaps*, she muses, *following the metaphor, I've been like a boat stuck on the shore. But at least a boat aground knows where it is. Safe.*

"Old boat," she says to herself, and goes into the front room and turns on the TV. It won't hurt to postpone thinking about this until *Frontline* is over. She rarely misses the show. Its moral stance, its unwillingness to accept the world's many shortcuts and dishonesties, reminds her of her father.

After dinner she makes herself a cup of tea, changes into a faded flannel nightgown, and settles into bed with her novel. She reads about women lovesick and betrayed, green with envy and childlike with hope, lifted up and cast down. I can't go through with all that, she thinks. There's a lot to be said for comfort: it's so much easier than passion. She turns off the bedside lamp.

Sleep won't come. She thinks about her possible promotion. She wonders if there is something too prideful about wishing for such a thing. But why? She has certainly worked hard enough—why shouldn't she enjoy the benefits? And then she recalls Charles's invitation. She catches herself drifting into a romantic fantasy and chides herself.

In the middle of the night she pads into the dark kitchen for a drink of water. Halfway across the cold tile floor she stops, arrested by the vision of a pilot light in the top of the stove, glowing like a tiny warm creature safe in its burrow.

* * *

When she returns from her second meeting on Monday morning, the message light on her phone is still not flashing. She places a stack of file folders on her desk and breathes a sigh of relief, complicated by a twinge of disappointment. The clock reads eleven-twenty. She looks back at the phone, steeling herself not to jump if it rings.

It would be much easier to react to a message than to have to speak to Charles Matthews directly, to explain why she hasn't called him back. If she knew what to say, it would make the conversation simpler, but she doesn't. Perhaps she should phone at lunchtime, so he won't be in and she can leave her own message, something neutral, noncommittal. But then, how neutral can she be? He asked her to dinner; he's expecting an answer. She knows she has to phone him soon; to not call would be rude. She picks up the file folders, drops them back down.

She rises, leaves her office, walks past a row of cubicles filled with secretaries clacking away at their computers. In the elevator bank, she stands absently stroking the collar of her jacket until she realizes she neglected to push the call button.

Inside the car, she grips the chrome rail behind her and stares blankly up at the ceiling. The elevators in the new Beardon Group building can sink forty-seven floors in less than a minute. Too fast. The door chimes and she steps out into the lobby slightly queasy, as if her soul has sunk below her body during the rapid descent. But then, she has felt like this all morning, subject to a nervous oscillation that has made it difficult to concentrate on her list of Things To Do.

She steps across the lobby, heels clicking on the marble floor, and buys a roll of Tums from the Pakistani man sitting on a stack of papers inside the newsstand. "How is your daughter?" she asks.

He beams. "Very good. She is starting at Hunter College very soon. Thank you for asking."

Grace nods and smiles.

Back in the elevator, the doors open at her floor, but she's reluctant to get out. She heads for the cafeteria instead.

They're serving her favorite lunch, a create-your-own stir-fry in which you point to raw ingredients and a chef sautées them in front of you, but she opts instead for a salad and some cottage cheese. Easier on the stomach. She joins the cashier's line behind two women, one of whom she recognizes as a very pregnant Candace Walker from Mr. Gibson's group. The other is a junior executive from the forty-fifth floor. They're so engrossed in their conversation that they don't turn around.

"I'm going to take maternity leave for a few months," Candace says, "but I guess I'll be in the market for some help after that."

"I've got a woman from Trinidad," the executive says. "She's incredibly reliable. I always know she's going to show up on time, and she's so quiet I hardly know she's around. And she has such good manners—I can see how that's rubbing off on my kids."

"I don't really like the idea of a stranger with my baby."

"Let me give you some advice: don't let the agency try to give you an American"—here Candace's companion lowers her voice—"you know, a black, because pretty soon you'll be dealing with a lot of no-show days, and you'll get tangled up in all sorts of family problems. They might want to borrow money, and if you do they'll just resent you for it. Trust me—it's a mess."

At this point, Candace turns around to survey the dining room, meets Grace's eyes, and comes up with a panicked attempt at a smile. Grace smiles back, as if to show that she hasn't heard anything at all.

And then she turns as if she's forgotten something and walks away with a rotten feeling deep in the pit of her stomach. She goes into the bathroom, closes the door of a stall behind her, and sits on a closed toilet seat. She's embarrassed and ashamed and mad at herself for not having said a word. But what could she have said?

After a moment she comes out of the stall, washes her hands, and rejoins the line.

* * *

The message light is blinking.

What does this man *want* of me? Grace asks. She picks up the phone and the little tin voice trapped inside announces "You have . . . three . . . new messages."

None of them is from Charles Matthews.

Again, like oil and water, this odd unsettled mix of disappointment and relief.

She leaves her office again, steps down to the kitchen at the end of the corridor for a diet soda. Crystal Farnsley and Angela Benitez, two secretaries from Mr. Perry's office, are sneaking a cigarette inside. They flush when she enters and slip out past her. She wishes she could stop them, ask for advice, but the look on their faces makes it clear how impossible that would be; like the other women in the office, they see her as responsible, efficient, serious. They might come to her for help with some work-related matter, but not to share any romantic confidences. Who would go to a spinster for dating advice?

Perhaps, she muses, she's as responsible as anyone for her isolation. All these years of telling herself that she was too busy to meet anyone outside of work—she should have gotten out more, made more of an effort to join in.

She looks at her reflection in the front of the soda machine: a crisp knee-length skirt and high-collared jacket, an ivory blouse buttoned primly at the neck. Crystal and Angela wear miniskirts, high heels, sexy stockings, plumage to attract some management bachelor, while she presents herself as earnest and respectable. A suit of armor. It's a wonder Charles Matthews has expressed interest at all. But then— with his graying hair, visible paunch, and arms held stiffly out from his sides as if suspended from the yoke of his shoulders—he's no Denzel Washington. Handsome nonetheless. Perhaps, it occurs to her now, he's nervous, too. Perhaps he has just returned from lunch and is staring down at his own telephone.

Supposing she says yes—supposing they have dinner and go out again and things develop into an actual romance. Then what if things go sour and she has to face him at some future business luncheon? Besides, with a possible promotion coming up, this is no time for even the appearance of impropriety.

She taps the button on the soda machine, watches the can clunk down into the trough, then heads back to her office, clicking the pull-tab.

On her desk lies a messengered manila envelope. Inside, she finds a DVD and a short note: "This is the film we discussed at the last board meeting. Thought you might enjoy it. Respectfully, Charles."

She sits and reads the note again.

On Barbados there had been a small yellow bird known as a *sugar bird*, in reference to the way it could be lured to a windowsill by a few sweet granules. I'm too big and too old to play at such foolishness, Grace thinks. Yet, despite herself, she smiles.

CHAPTER EIGHT

Halfway down the block, Melba Wilson props her foot up against a fire hydrant. Her heel feels raw. She reaches down and pries off a new winter boot. Digs in her purse in search of a Band-aid. She considers turning back to the house, but if she's late with dinner, her son Jamel will start talking about going off to McDonald's with his friends. To eat the greasy fried junk that is killing black people by the millions.

At the corner of Smith Street she steps into the vestibule of the Bayamon Savings Bank to use the ATM. "Do you want a record of this transaction?" the screen asks when she's done. "No," she punches. Doesn't want to see that balance. No news is good news. She peers around the alcove at the desk of Mr. Rodriguez, supervisor of her mortgage. Oh, God, she thinks, don't let me be called in to see him. With business hurting as it is at the real estate office, that day may come all too soon.

She chews her bottom lip: if only the rich white people would find some other neighborhood to colonize.

She strides back out onto the sidewalk, favoring her left foot. She stops to check out a rack of baby clothes parked on the sidewalk in front of a Puerto Rican clothing shop. *Desiree's Fashions*. A big handwritten sign proclaims Everything Fifty Percent Off. Frowning, she pushes the little outfits along the rack. She rubs the fabric between her fingers, squints down at the stitching. Inexpensive yes, but cheaply made. Too cheap for her grandchild.

Moving on, she passes a new sushi restaurant and a French bistro with entrées—she notices from the menu—costing up to twenty dollars. On Smith Street! It seems like almost every week a bodega or candy shop is replaced by some fancy new restaurant frequented by white people in expensive-looking clothes.

Inside the supermarket she loads a cart, humming along with the Muzak. "My Girl" by the Temptations. In the paper goods aisle, she pauses in the middle of reaching out for a stack of cups, struck by a vivid memory.

She was setting out cups and plates on a card table down in the basement—it must have been the late seventies. And her husband James—*James plus Melba equals "Jamel"*—was behind her, reaching his stout arm around the middle of her crepe dress, pressing his lips to the back of her neck before the guests came, swaying to a song just like this. They had some *parties* then. A barbecue one Fourth of July that lasted from noon until the next morning. Al Green and Marvin Gaye. Earth, Wind, and Fire. Slowdancing under a dim red light bulb, getting it on to Barry White in the wee hours. Dancing in the old house they'd spent years fixing up. There were black neighbors all along the block then, and they visited in each other's homes and sat out in the gardens in the summertime. Not like now, after so many of her friends have been pushed out by rising rents or disappearing jobs.

In the checkout line, she waits behind an Arab woman and her two daughters. *Look at those shawls*, Melba says to herself. *I don't know how they can stand it in the summertime*. Their conversation sounds harsh and guttural. The Korean girl behind the register smiles broadly.

The Arab woman reaches into her canvas shoulder bag and pulls out a handful of food stamps. *Well*, Melba thinks, *I guess you're Americans now*. She herself has never used a food stamp in her life. Although, God knows, with the noises the bank is making about foreclosure, after she's been a good customer for over twenty years . . . No. It won't come to that. She won't let it.

She turns away. Farther back in line, a young white couple is leaning against a cart. They look familiar. Oh, yes, the new neighbors, two doors down. Wearing clothes out of some camping and fishing catalog. She grins fiercely to herself: not a lot of camping and fishing around here.

She turns back to find the Arab woman pushing *her* food backward on the conveyor.

"What you think you're doing?"

The Arab woman looks blank, pretending she doesn't know what's what.

"Don't go touching people's food," Melba says. "That's not the way we do things here."

Out on the sidewalk again, she pauses. The sight of the baby clothes has put her in mind to get something for her granddaughter. Something nice, not like the shabby outfits Tisha's *other* grandmother dresses her in. She considers walking over to Macy's, in the mall, but it's cold out and her foot is paining her so . . . There's a place up on Court Street. Not a place she would go to normally, but it *is* nearby.

She limps up the block toward Court, past a chain-link fence and a schoolyard full of screaming kids. Dodgeball. Imagine: they still play that. There's a good life lesson: it's better to be the one throwing the ball than the one trapped in the middle. For sixteen years she has fought to spare her son any of the hardships she herself lived through. Her little-girl self, crowded into a tiny basement apartment on Chicago's South Side with four brothers and sisters. One time she lay in bed for a week with an infected tooth swelling the whole side of her face because her mother couldn't afford the dentist. Tougher than the pain itself had been watching her mother weeping, helpless.

She turns onto Court Street. In the bay window of a fancy new coffee shop, a blackboard advertises the specials of the day: Leek and Fennel Soup. Foccacia with Roasted Vegetables. Inside, several young white people lounge about and type on little computers.

Next door, a colorful custom-painted sign hangs over the storefront. *Emily & Josh*. A bell tinkles as she opens the door. The shop is bright and sunny, filled with racks of colorful little outfits. A young white woman at the counter glances up and says a cheery hello, but Melba is sure there was a slight pause between the look and the greeting, and she knows what that means. *We don't get many of you people in here.*

She gives only the slightest of nods in acknowledgment, then moves away to look at the clothes.

The bell over the door tinkles again. A young white woman comes in towing a little boy of three or four. "*Mommy*," the child whines. "You *said* I could get the video."

The mother kneels down in front of the boy and patiently says, "Now honey, I told you we don't have time to go to the video store right now. We have to go pick up Daddy at the gym. Maybe later we can stop by the health food store and get you a nice carrot juice and your favorite—tofu cheesecake."

The boy twists away. "No! Video!"

The mother continues talking, as if reasoning with a miniature adult.

Melba turns away in disgust.

* * *

Crouched on the edge of the beanbag chair down in the basement of his house, Jamel works on maintaining his Air Jordans. As he pulls the old laces out, the tips slip through the eyelets like spaghetti being suctioned into a mouth. Before he inserts new ones, he picks up a toothbrush standing in a mug of warm water and tenderly scrubs the leather clean.

Scrunching back into the chair, he smooths his palm over a duct tape patch. In the corner, the barbecue grill stands forlorn, waiting for summer. Across the room, an ancient Day-Glo poster of Bruce Lee in fighting stance curls down off the wall. Time moves too slow in the cold weather. If the temperature was just a few degrees warmer or the wind a little less brisk, he'd be standing out on the stoop like a fisherman on the bank of a river, waiting to see what the passing traffic might bring. In the winter he's cut off from the street, the source of action, of possibility. He'll be trapped inside with his mother, listening to her press him about getting a job, or finishing high school. Time stretches ahead, intolerable.

Christmas is approaching and his mother's all moody, as she gets every year at this time, remembering how his father died. Twelve years ago on Christmas Day, James Wilson was standing in the kitchen opening a can of pineapple rings; he paused to complain of a pain in his chest, set the opener carefully down, staggered away from the counter, and fell back into a corner, his head making a hollow thunk against the door of the dishwasher as he fell. Jamel, four at the time, knelt by the body. Uncertain if this was supposed to be a joke, he reached out to pat his dad's plump shoulder.

He slips his favorite DXZ Crew CD into his boombox. Time parsed out in the bass beats, controlled, mastered. He settles back in the chair, soothed by the way the music roots him in the present, clears his head of the thoughts crowding in. He opens the cover and studies a photo: Darius, Vic Tha BigHead, Young Chocky and the other DXZ rappers standing defiant in a vacant lot.

He turns the volume all the way up. DXZ Crew slams out of the boombox, the sound so strong and raw it distorts the little speakers. If he can just convince his mother to pay for his new system from the Mall, he'll be able to get clear sound at any volume.

* * *

"What time she gettin' off?" he asks, nodding toward Onica perched on her stool behind the counter of Video Magic.

Tree looks up at the clock in the back. " 'bout an hour."

"We gonna wait?"

"I'm waitin'. You can leave if you want."

Jamel shrugs. "Ah'ight." He doesn't go anywhere, though—just roams around gazing at the rows of videos stretched out under the fluorescent lights. He glances back at Onica, looking cute on her stool, and Tree, resting his big arms on the counter while he talks to his girlfriend in his shy, earnest way. That's what *his* life should be like, mooning around a girlfriend all day, no worries about kids and responsibilities. It's not fair: he had just a year or two to try to figure out how to act around girls, and then suddenly he was a father. And

Shanice doesn't want anything to do with him now, sex-wise. Tree says he should check out some new girls—"You ain't young but the one time"—but he already has enough to worry about.

Thanks to the new manager, the store radio is tuned to a salsa station; the frenetic rhythm is giving Jamel a headache. The music finally stops for a commercial, some manic announcer booming away in Spanish. Jamel grins at the way the occasional English word seems to jump out of the foreign stew. "*Sieche cinquo dias habada habada* Burger King! *Habada habada habada* Preparation H!"

He wanders back to the front counter. A young white business-man-type with a canvas bag over his shoulder moves slowly up the center aisle. He glances anxiously around the store, turning to watch who's coming in.

"What's he gettin'?" Jamel asks Onica. The girl has an uncanny ability to predict her customers' tastes.

She barely looks up. "Bootie," she mutters, just loud enough for her friends to hear. "He checkin' if the neighbors gonna see him."

Sure enough, the guy hands over a box for an X-rated movie. Jamel glimpses a photo on the cover of a naked woman licking her own nipple. Onica goes in the back and retrieves the video, briskly scans the bar code, and slips it into a bag, avoiding eye contact with the customer throughout the whole transaction. Jamel has noticed that she's fastidious: she always sets the change on the counter rather than touch the customer's hand.

Sometimes, on days when she's not on duty, he sneaks down to the Adult section in the basement to quickly scan the boxes, with their raw photos and crude titles. *Pretty 'n Pink. Nasty Asses.* Sex, it seems to him, is a mystery, lodged in a shameful basement room of the mind.

The front door swings open and Frankie the owner strides in, tan even in winter, wearing his usual black turtleneck and gold chain, running his palm over his razor-shaved hair. Out through the front window, Jamel can see his brand-new red Trans Am parked on Smith Street.

"You badass niggers better get away from the counter," Frankie says, with just enough of a sarcastic smile to defuse the slur. "You gonna scare all my customers away."

"Aay, yo," says Tree, doing his Vinnie Barbarino impression. "Were you up the street doing some bidniss wit' the Godfathah?"

Frankie grins as he moves behind the counter. "Awright, you punks. Why don't you leave girlfriend alone here so she can do some work for once in her life?"

Jamel and his friend wander off down an aisle, idly checking out the new releases. Tree looks around and lowers his voice. "Yo, son, you wanna get in on some easy green?"

Jamel looks up. "Doin' what?"

"You know that house acrost from Building Two, where Tito and his boys got their crib?"

Jamel frowns. Often, on the way to visit friends on the other side of the projects, he has walked past the house and the lookout perched on the stoop, the man's head swiveling from side to side like a jittery bird. Though he's never been inside or tried the product, Jamel knows that there's an apartment on the second floor where you can buy as many vials of crack as you want. "Ready rock," the lookout mutters as potential customers walk by. "We got blue, we got Mahals." Little plastic caps skitter away on the sidewalk underfoot, royal blue or in the shape of tiny crowns.

Tree notes Jamel's dark look and throws his hands up in the air. "Son, I'm *tellin'* you—it's the easiest fuckin' money you could ever see. All you gotta do is stand outside. You can even listen to your Walkmans."

Jamel looks away. "Why you wanna mess with that shit?"

"I need the money, son. Straight up."

"Ah'ight. Then why would I wanna mess wit it?"

"We could get us a *ride*," Tree answers. "Th'ow some speakers in the back, get outta this jive-ass place. See somethin' new for a change."

Jamel can picture that, too. Sitting in a brand new Lexus with tinted windows, listening to the bass thumping. Getting away. He sighs. He doesn't need the money. He can understand why his friend might want to get involved with this lookout business, since he has no mother to deal with and less to lose, but he himself has a solid situation at home;

his mother gives him what he wants. Come Christmas, or soon after, he'll have his new sound system and everybody in the neighborhood will come by the house to check it out.

They fall silent as someone walks down the aisle, the new white neighbor, who always carries a briefcase. Jamel looks away as if he hasn't seen the man. He picks up a video box and sets it down. "What about the Five-Ohs?"

"What they gonna do? Even if they catch you—number one, you ain't got no priors. Two, you ain't carryin' nothin'. You ain't sellin' nothin'. They gonna send you up for standing on a stoop?"

Jamel shakes his head. He knows that Tree has chosen to make this job seem simpler than it is, to minimize the risk.

Tree snorts in disgust. "Some G' you gonna be, always worried about your Moms and shit."

Jamel, wounded by this direct hit, walks away.

"Candy-ass motherfucker," Tree calls after him.

Jamel turns back, a pained look on his face. "Yo, why you wanna be like that? How many times we help you out?"

Tree, who spends half of his life over at his friend's house, takes a hit of his own. He sighs, shrugs. "Forget about it, then."

"Let's go visit my system," Jamel says.

They leave the store and walk toward the mall.

*　*　*

Later, Jamel throws his coat over the banister and starts up toward his room, but pauses when he hears his mother's voice from the kitchen.

"Jamel, where you been, baby?"

"Stop calling me baby."

"I didn't hear you."

He changes course and walks down the hall to the kitchen, where she sits at the table clipping coupons.

"I said, stop calling me baby."

She eyes him shrewdly. "Oh, you a big man now?"

He crosses to the refrigerator and peers inside. Listless, he closes the door without taking anything out. "Big enough."

"So where you been, Mr. Big?"

He doesn't want to aggravate her, so he lets the dig pass without comment. "I was over at the Mall. Checking out my system."

His mother squints with concentration as she cuts out another coupon. "You ain't never tell me how much this thing gonna cost."

He shrugs nervously, walks back to the refrigerator, rests his hand on the door.

"Jamel?"

"They got a layaway."

His mother adds the coupon to a stack on the table. "How much?"

"Twelve hundred," he mutters, almost inaudibly.

His mother looks up sharply, scissors poised in mid-air. "Say again?"

"We got up to a year to pay it off."

"I don't care if we got a lifetime. I said I would buy you a stereo, not the whole store. What you thinkin'? It's hard enough to meet these mortgage payments every month without buyin' you some solid gold stereo."

"I could help."

She snorts. "With what?"

"I could get a job."

"You could get a job," she repeats dubiously. "If you can help save up twelve hundred dollars, then you can help do right by your daughter. And you should be saving up some money for college."

He rolls his eyes. "Don't start that shit up again."

"What did you say?"

"Nothin'. How you think I'm'a get into college? Can't go to college without no high school diploma."

"What does that tell you?"

"Tells me I best start making some money if I want that system." He grabs a Dr. Pepper from the fridge and scoots out of the room.

To fight the first big snow of the season, city workers crisscross Brooklyn, scattering tons of salt. The stuff melts, seeps down through manholes into blind buried arteries, gnaws through insulation into living wire. Flames bloom in the dark. Water boils to steam, irresistible in force.

Poonk! An iron manhole cover springs up toward a streetlight like a thumb-flipped bottle cap. Raw fire follows, to lap the bumper of a parked Dodge van.

Poonk! Another manhole blows.

Sirens wail and flashing lights slap window shades tinged TV blue. Doors open and people stumble out onto their stoops, shirts unbuttoned, shoelaces overflowing. Down the dark block they come, pulling on jackets, single figures, couples, parents towing children by the hand, moving toward the lights as to a bonfire, drawing together, faces lit by fear and joy.

CHAPTER NINE

ARRIVING AT HER CUBICLE, CAROL SLINGS HER PURSE ONTO HER desk, opens a paper bag, and sets out her usual deli breakfast: coffee black, two sugars; toasted poppy bagel with just a dab of cream cheese. She fishes a cassette out of the *In* file, slips the tape into the Dictaphone, clamps on her headset, and the day begins.

Mr. Burkett's rheumy, hesitant voice: "Hello, Carol, these are . . . just a few responses . . . to some internship applications. Please fill in the names . . . on the usual *No* form. Thank you. I should be back from Chicago . . . around noon Wednesday. Hold down the fort."

Indeed she will. Recently Mr. Burkett, founder and senior statesman of Burkett, Christensen, & Chang, has been losing his memory. If she didn't cover for him, remembering his appointments and coming up with excuses for the ones he still manages to miss, the firm would have lost a great deal of business over the past few years. In recognition of her publicly unacknowledgeable role as linchpin of the office, Mr. Christensen and Mr. Chang have discreetly made sure that she gets a sizable raise every year.

In the earphones Mr. Burkett clears his throat and something clatters loudly. Probably his dentures falling on his desk, she thinks; smiles.

"Hey, Fasone, what's the joke?"

She turns to find Tom McGlynn from Accounting leaning against the cubicle, his paunch resting on top of the low wall. McGlynn often takes a break to stroll around the office—he reminds her of a patrol cop with an easy beat.

"Didn't I tell you not to sneak up on me, you bum?"

"*Me dispiace, signora.*" His boyish face opens wide. "Hey, wanna hear a joke? D'ya hear about the salesman who got tired of using his finger to make his calls? He used his—"

"Dick-to-phone," Carol finishes. She snorts at her colleague's deflated face. "You told us that one last week. You're a poor excuse for a human being, McGlynn."

"That's funny," he replies mock-dolefully. "That's exactly what my ex-wife always told me. Speaking of which, how's your Hungarian refugee?"

"He's *Bosnian*. And he's fine, thank you very much."

"When are you going to leave him and run away with me? We'll cash in our Four-oh-one-Ks and fly down to Acapulco together—"

"Where were you all those years before I got married?" she asks.

Awkward silence. You never flirted when I was single, she thinks, watching as he fiddles nervously with a plastic pinwheel attached to her office-supply carousel. Where were you when I was so lonely I would have begged for a date, when I was just big old homely Carol Fasone in the secretarial pool? It's safe to play the big Romeo now, isn't it, when there's no chance I might say yes.

She feels bad for McGlynn all of a sudden, standing there looking so embarrassed. Funny how the tables have turned, him being the lonely one now.

"Anyhow," she says, "my husband is only one step away from becoming a full U.S. citizen. He's getting his green card today—he's free and clear to stay now."

"You gonna celebrate?"

"Amy's gonna cover my phone this afternoon so I can go shopping and get home early. I'm gonna surprise him with a special dinner. Hey—the girls are going out to Manganaro's for lunch today. Wanna come with?"

McGlynn pretends to think it over, but she can see he's pleased at the prospect of company.

"Why the hell not?" He walks away singing, "Nothing could be finah than to be in Carol-lina in the mo-oo-o-rnin'."

She shakes her head, turns on her computer, and boots up the template for the internship rejections. An hour later she pulls a pack of cigarettes out of her purse, but decides not to take a break. I don't need any gimmicks to make it through this day, she thinks. Not with so much to look forward to at the end of it.

* * *

"Hey, what'll it be for the Missus?"

Up on Court Street Joe Faiucco stands behind the counter of his butcher shop, as his father did when Joe and Carol were in high school together. He has his dad's good looks, too: the distinguished, prematurely silver hair, the fine-chiseled face, like a Roman statue.

"Give me a pound and a half of your finest lamb," Carol says, full of plans for this most special dinner.

"Leg or chops?"

"Chops. Cut 'em thick, would you? I want 'em nice for my husband." Even after two years the words give her a proprietary pleasure: *my husband*. She's a part of this community, a wife.

Joe claps his hands together. "Wait'll you see what I got. *Beeyuteeful*."

While he disappears into the back of the shop, Carol surveys the strings of garlic hanging like braids from the ceiling, the sun-dried tomatoes in murky oil in a jar on the counter, the Calamata olives shining darkly from a crock. Once when she was a little girl, Mr. Faiucco Sr. offered her an olive and laughed at her grimace of distaste. Sometimes, though, he'd give her a rice ball, and on the walk home with her mother she'd bite carefully through the thin brown crust, savoring the warm garlicky mush of rice, peas, and ground meat inside, trying to make the good taste last all the way home.

Joe Jr. emerges from the back, bearing four beautiful chops on a sheet of waxed paper, like a prize.

On the way home, Carol stops in at Annatto's Bakery for a loaf sprinkled with sesame seeds ("How are ya muthah's lungs?" asks Maria Annatto behind the counter); into Court Liquors for a bottle of chardonnay ("Special occasion?" asks Frank Bennedetto); into the Carroll Gardens Pastry Shop for a box of chocolate cannolis ("I seen ya husband walkin' by yestihday," says Angie Costarella). Outside the Off-Track Betting office several old gents in tweed caps call out as she hurries past, asking her to send their regards to her mother.

* * *

"Ma? Milosz?"

She sets her shopping bags on the kitchen counter and calls out into the hollow house. Without waiting for a reply, she walks into the hall and climbs the stairs. She almost bumps into a pair of thick-stockinged legs and looks up, startled.

"Jesus, Ma, you scared the hell out of me! Why didn't you answer when I—Ma, what's the matter?"

Her mother, sitting at the top of the staircase, presses a liver-spotted hand over her chest. She's sniffling. "Carrie, please. Don't come up here."

Carol stands, her foot poised on the edge of the landing. "What, are you crazy? What's going on?" She looks into her mother's face. "Ma, are you sick?" Her mother shakes her head fearfully. "Is it Milosz? Is he all right?"

"*Don't*," is all her mother can manage. The old woman slumps against the railing.

Carol's mind whirls. What could be so terrible that her mother doesn't want her to go up to the bedroom? A jagged image flashes into her mind, Milosz hanging from the metal rod in the clothes closet. No, he wouldn't—no matter what terrible news he might have received from home, he wouldn't harm himself. Not with all his plans, with all they have together—

She rushes past her mother crumpled on the landing, bursts into the bedroom. No Milosz.

She turns, dazed, and the details she missed on her headlong dash into the room sting her like wasps. No grubby sneakers tossed beside the bed. No neckties flung over the knob of the bathroom door. She bends down, flips the bedspread up off the floor, and peers under the bed: no suitcase.

She turns back to the closet, emptied, on this day of her husband's gaining his permanent residence status, of all his clothes.

CHAPTER TEN

"HUH?" MITCHELL RAISES HIS FACE FROM WHERE IT LIES SMUSHED against a corner of the pillow.

"Go back to sleep," his wife mumbles. "It's nothing."

Somewhere out in the dark streets, the faint *Wah!-Oh Wah!-Oh* of a police siren swells to a crescendo and then shifts away. Mitchell rolls onto his back and puts a hand over his heart. The window shade brightens with a white light that seems to be coming from above. Still groggy with sleep, he realizes that the dopplered *Throp-throp-throp* he hears is a helicopter circling over the block.

He rises and pads across the house to the back window, peers out to see a floodlight shining down over the courtyard. He thinks of a TV cop show, envisions a pilot's-eye-view of some fleeing criminal frantically scrambling over fences, caught in a circle of glaring light. *Good*, he thinks: catch the bastards. The light swings away over the rooftops, leaving the courtyard dark and still.

Back in bed, he rolls over, reaches an arm over Kristin's sleep-logged body, and presses his face into the crook of her warm neck.

* * *

Early the next day on the way to the gym, he barely pauses when he reaches the spot where his mugging took place. Heaps of snow, gritty with black exhaust, are banked against the curb. A few images flick through his mind—a dark figure darting out between two parked cars, a strange curved knife—but their hold over his nervous system has weakened considerably. Even the day after the assault, when he returned to the spot, which had grown in his imagination into some terrible mythic arena, he'd been surprised to find only a matter-of-fact stretch of asphalt. (At night, though, the place retains some power, as he can tell by a quickening under his ribs, a clamminess of his upper lip.)

He turns the corner onto Smith Street. On this Sunday morning only a few loners are out, drifting along the sidewalks, dazed. Mitchell strides past humble three-story brick façades bearing tacky awnings; past a sign with raised plastic letters for a butcher shop, scrawny yellow chickens hanging in the window; a cramped medical building offering the services of a dentist, a podiatrist, a gynecologist. The sound of a subway train rumbles up through a grate beneath his feet.

Three teenagers in hooded coats stare into the window of a store, some sort of Army-Navy place. Mitchell waits until they do their junior-tough-guy walk down the street, rocking from side to side as if suspended by wires, then steps forward to see what held their attention. It wouldn't have been the orange poncho, or the metallic space blanket . . . He looks down: the floor of the display is covered with a geometric pattern, radiating arcs of ninja knives, brass knuckles, canisters of mace. He groans: Jesus, just what the neighborhood needs.

A sharp voice at his elbow causes him to look around. A stocky, red-faced woman wearing a bleached denim outfit walks by, talking to another woman in a white motorcycle jacket.

The woman raises a meaty fist. "I tole that fat fuckin' whore that if she ever comes around my house again lookin' for my husband, I'm gonna come up on her and snap her back like a turkey bone!" She shakes her head for emphasis; a ratty ponytail sticks out over the collar of her coat.

"You got a right," the friend agrees solemnly, brows raised over blue-shadowed eyes. "I wouldn't blame you one bit."

Mitchell turns up the hill toward his gym, contemplating what it would take to make him capable of such violence. After the mugging he has been able to imagine it, but the thought of pain, disfigurement—an eye poked out, a nose broken—makes him cringe.

* * *

In the gym he jogs down into the men's locker room, with its smell of disinfectant, dank towels, dirty sneakers. It takes him a minute to find an empty locker, but when he does, he can't fully open the door unless he claims some space from a huge black guy who's pulling his clothes from the adjoining locker.

"Excuse me," Mitchell mumbles.

His neighbor doesn't reply, but shifts slightly out of the way.

Mitchell carefully swings the door of his locker open and stows his jacket inside. Though there's another gym closer to his house, he joined the Brooklyn Athletic Club because he assumed that the place—due to its location in the expensive heart of Brooklyn Heights—would be similar to his former gym on the upper East Side; that it would be filled with young professionals like himself. And it is, mostly, young guys in college sweatshirts spotting for one another in the weight room, grim-faced blondes on the treadmills, leotards disappearing into their perfect little butt cheeks as they run, run, run.

He's unprepared for this moment, though, standing here pulling his shirt off next to this man with massive, muscle-bunched shoulders gleaming under the fluorescent lights—the guy's built like Mike Tyson, for chrissakes. Mitchell prides himself on a worldly racial tolerance, but it occurs to him that—aside from riding the subway—he hasn't spent much time this close to a black man. Not a half-naked one, that's for sure. There's one young black trader in the office, but he grew up in Scarsdale and talks like a California surfer dude.

Another black guy lumbers in, thigh muscles stout as telephone poles. He wears big prescription goggles like Magic Johnson.

"Yo, whussup?" he asks Mitchell's neighbor, slapping the guy's palm and moving smoothly into the fraternal handshake that Mitchell tried the other day with a guy in the mailroom at work, feeling like a complete fraud.

"Man, you catch the game last night?" the guy with goggles says. "Motherfuckin' Marbury was all over Philadelphia's shit!"

"Word up," his buddy replies.

Mitchell changes into his squash gear, listening to these guys discuss basketball, pondering their profoundly muscular bodies. How often does he see a flabby black guy in a gym? They never seem to have that after-work blurriness, that desk-job softness he fights in himself. He sits on a stool to tie his sneakers, then rubs his hands together, proud of the calluses that years of holding a squash racquet have given him. And he is proud of how, through sheer willpower, he has managed to transform himself into the athlete he'd never dreamed he could be, that skinny kid in junior high who could barely do a single pull-up.

He lifts his head and discovers that the tenor of the discussion has shifted.

"When's your court date?" the guy with goggles asks his buddy.

"I'm supposed to go in for some preliminary bullshit on the tenth. I'm gonna get crushed, I can tell. What about you?"

"I have to go in on Monday."

Mitchell freezes. He's sitting here with two giant black guys talking about their court appearances. What are they charged with?

Recently, walking down Smith Street, he noticed a big somber building rising over Atlantic Avenue, with a strange wire cage on the roof. A sign revealed that the building's a jail, the Brooklyn House of Detention, and the cage—he could just make out by craning his neck all the way back—encloses a rooftop basketball court. Perhaps these two brawny guys will be continuing their conversation up there in a couple of weeks.

"Who's your judge?" says the guy with goggles.

"I think it's gonna be Hardwick."

"Damn, she's hard all right. You better get your motherfuckin' act together before you walk in there."

"My case is pretty tight."

"You better hope so. Hardwick's thing is to quash subpoenas during the pretrial conference."

Mitchell relaxes, sheepish. They're *lawyers*.

* * *

Twenty minutes later, he's the one doing the cursing.

His opponent is a young Pakistani-American guy, a diagnostician in the oncology ward over at Long Island City Hospital. He's short, wiry, and cheerful, decked out in impeccable whites. The man wears a knee brace. Even with this handicap he appears to be a better player, planted firmly in the middle of the court while Mitchell lurches all over the place chasing a flurry of rail shots, then *Wha-pang!* catching him off guard with a sneaky boast shot that caroms directly off the wall into the opposite corner.

"Fuck!" Mitchell shouts. He fans the neck of his soggy polo shirt, turns to scoop the ball up onto his racquet and flip it to the other player. What's fraying his temper is that the guy is so friendly and self-effacing: he apologizes for each point, making excuses for Mitchell—"the floor was just waxed," "the light in this court is too bright." They play on, the high-ceilinged court echoing their ragged breath and the squeak of their tennis shoes on the floor.

Mitchell lifts his goggles and wipes away some salty sweat. Through the Plexiglas rear wall of the court, he sees that an audience has gathered in the waiting area. He hates that: the game should be a simple, focused world, everything stripped down to this bright room, two men engaged in elemental combat. Now he feels like an aquarium fish on display. An uncomfortable memory rises. Back when he used to play tennis in high school, the other kids would tease him for the hot tears that sprang to his eyes when he lost a match. He couldn't help it: the humiliation of knowing that his father was frowning in disgust from the sidelines was just too much. Afterward, his father wouldn't say anything to him, and somehow that was worse than if he did.

He rallies, grimly determined that this time he's going to come out on top. A fierce determination guides his forehand; he sees the onlookers flinch when—*crack!*—his racquet hits the Plexiglas as he manages a diving save. The Pakistani guy is running now.

Mitchell wins the match by two points.

"Good game, man," his rival says, shaking his hand earnestly.

"You would've beat me, normally," Mitchell replies, ashamed of how he made the guy work with his bum knee.

* * *

That night, the phone jolts him out of sleep. He turns, heart hammering, to decipher the glowing hands of the bedside clock. Three a.m. A phone call at this hour can only mean someone has died. His wife's father, with his clogged arteries or, God forbid, his own mother . . . He lifts the receiver to hear a vaguely familiar raspy voice.

"Sorry to wake you at this hour," the man says, though he doesn't sound particularly sorry. "This is Detective Schimek, down at the precinct. We got a couple of youths sitting here that we'd like you to come down and see if you can identify."

"Now?" Mitchell asks, still groggy. "Can't I come down first thing in the morning?"

"I'm sorry, but it has to be now. These kids haven't been charged, so we can't hold 'em very long."

"I'm not too sure about going out into the streets at this hour."

"Don't worry—I'll swing by and pick you up. Half an hour."

Mitchell dresses, then stares out the window until an unmarked car pulls up under a streetlight. It's freezing out; as he steps down off the stoop, he wishes he'd thought to put on more clothes. A woman is sitting in the front seat with Schimek, so he bows into the back.

"This is Mrs. Harvey," Schimek says, introducing him to the middle-aged black woman. "She was robbed two blocks away Sunday night, and her description sounds like it matches your boys."

Despite the late hour, Mrs. Harvey has taken the effort to dress with care and Mitchell feels self-conscious about his loose shirttails. During the ride he overhears the woman tell the detective that she works as a registrar at City College.

Inside the station house, while Mrs. Harvey waits, Mitchell follows the detective into a little narrow room with a pane of opaque glass set into a wall. Once the door is shut the detective turns off the light and taps against the glass. On the other side, a curtain pulls back and suddenly Mitchell can see into another room, where six young black men sit lined up, the mug-shot book come to life. One has a gash crusted with barely-dried blood over his bloodshot left eye. Another has a scar running down the side of his neck. Most of the youths look down with dazed, resigned expressions, but a couple glare defiantly at the window. Mitchell steps back.

"Don't worry," the detective says. "It's a mirror in there—they can't see you. Take your time." He raps the glass. One by one a cop leads each suspect to stand a couple of feet from the window. Despite Mitchell's invisibility he flinches as each youth comes near.

After all the suspects have approached the window he turns to Schimek and shakes his head. None of these faces is right; none matches the fading memory of two smooth young faces shining under a streetlamp.

Schimek leads him from the room and goes back inside with Mrs. Harvey.

Mitchell waits in a bleak fluorescent-lit lounge. He would have expected to feel unalloyed hatred for this row of possible muggers, but these young men, for the most part, don't seem like willful delinquents—they look beaten down, wretched, like prisoners of war. His father could just have said that they're too lazy to work, but it occurs to Mitchell that there's something else going on here—that maybe these crimes are a way of expressing frustration, of doing battle. Against whom? Not him, specifically, but—like it or not—he represents the enemy. He shifts uncomfortably in the rigid chair as—for the first time in his life—he sincerely wonders: how did this situation come to pass?

Later, following a second lineup, he sits bleary-eyed in the lounge with Mrs. Harvey, drinking stale coffee from a paper cup.

Schimek calls him over to a desk in the corner. "I wanna ask you one more time—you're positive none of those kids looked familiar at all?"

"Positive. Those guys you showed me were all messed up, gangster-looking, and the ones who robbed me were young, like eighteen or nineteen, good-looking kids."

Schimek glances at Mrs. Harvey perched tiredly on the edge of a cracked vinyl sofa and lowers his voice. "Mister, I been doing this job twenty-four years and I've never seen a good-looking brother."

Mitchell is taken aback by Schimek's remark—he winces at the way the detective assumes that he'll appreciate it, his locker-room certainty that they're on the same "team"—but this man is his protector. His wince twists into an uneasy smile.

Outside, in the hush of night, they settle into Schimek's car and drive back along the silent avenues. Ahead, the lights of the Wysocki Houses rise over Mitchell's dark sleeping street.

CHAPTER ELEVEN

"For starters, tonight we have a nice *zuppa di clams*. Also, a very nice *prosciutt'* with melon . . ."

The waiter stands by the table staring up at a fixed point above his head as he recites the evening's specials. He looks, Grace thinks, like a young saint having a mystical experience in some religious painting. She tries to concentrate, despite her awareness of Charles Matthews, who sits across the candlelit table in a stiff but friendly pose, hands clasped on the table, distinguished white-haired head cocked toward the waiter. Although she has watched the man eat quite a few board dinners, this is only the second time she has sat down to eat with him.

"For *ensalata*, we have a nice arugula with warm goat cheese," the waiter drones on. "We also have a very nice *bruschetta* with tomatoes and olive oil . . ." He looks about seventeen.

So far Grace and Charles have met twice in Manhattan, once for dinner and once to see an off-Broadway play. For this third date he said that he wanted to try a Brooklyn restaurant. She glances over his shoulder at a mural depicting some earthy Italian town clumped on a hillside over an aquamarine sea. Above the painting, a bright twinkling string of Christmas tree lights runs across the top of the wall and drapes down over a tree bearing little oranges. She's relieved to notice a young black couple sitting at a table by the front door: this means that she and her date are not breaking new ground by coming here. Carroll Gardens is a very close-knit Italian neighborhood, not exactly famous for openness to the neighboring black communities in Red Hook and Boerum Hill. Grace remembers that when she first moved to the area, looking for an apartment, she heard that sometimes elderly Italians with apartments to rent would not advertise the fact publicly, for that very reason. She was nervous enough about the date without having to worry whether they'd be given a frosty reception in the restaurant. So far, though, they seem to be receiving the same courteous treatment as the other patrons. We certainly look respectable, she thinks. Maybe *too* respectable. She has tried to dress in a casual way, but still ended up looking as if she's on her way to a business dinner: a skirted purple suit, a white blouse with a high collar, a string of pearls. And though Charles has left behind his usual gray suit, he has traded it for a dark blue one. She glances around at the other couples in the restaurant, who seem relaxed in casual clothes.

Over in the corner she spies her new neighbors, the Bretts. The young man—Mitchell, she believes his name is—wears a denim button-down shirt. His wife, in jeans, has a model's good looks and an almost severe aura of self-possession. They don't seem to have a great deal to say to each other.

". . . We have a nice linguine with fresh clam sauce, also a very nice *braciole* served with a side of linguine . . ."

Grace curbs a wry smile. It seems that there are two basic food groups here at Michelangelo's: "nice" and "very nice." The list goes on and on. A nice red snapper . . . A very nice veal rollatini . . . As the waiter struggles to retrieve the last couple of menu items from the ether, she suppresses an urge to laugh.

Charles, in his calm Southern accent, orders a bottle of cabernet and says that they'll need a few minutes to decide. "Did you get all that?" he asks Grace as the young man—relieved to have made it through his recitation—slips away.

"I was too busy being impressed by his memory," she says, grinning. "They might as well ask the poor boy to recite all of *Hamlet*."

The kid glides back, bearing the bottle of wine. Grace looks on with interest as her date considers the label and follows the rest of the wine-opening ritual. After the waiter fills their glasses and goes off to the kitchen with their orders, Charles leans forward conspiratorially. "To tell you the truth, I'm not really sure what that's all about. As long as it's wine, I'm happy."

Based upon the way he savored the first testing sip, Grace suspects that he may know a lot about the subject, but she appreciates his attempt to defuse the continuing awkwardness and formality of their dates.

A busboy steps forward bearing a napkin-covered basket. Charles picks it up and offers it to her. She reaches inside, then jerks her hand away.

"Are you okay?" he asks, eyebrows knitted in concern.

She laughs. "The bread is hot."

He smiles, and she feels a tension begin to release in her shoulders. She raises her head as if to speak, but—smiling—shakes it instead. "I keep starting to call you 'Mister Matthews'."

"No, *please*. Call me 'Charles.' Or 'Chuck,' if you like. Otherwise, I'll have to call you 'Miz Howard,' and then where will we be?"

Where indeed? What does this man want from her? Twenty or even ten years ago she might have suspected a simple sexual attraction—which she would probably have avoided, if not for personal, then for professional reasons—but he seems so *solid*, so respectable. Like a family man.

"Do you have any children?" she asks.

He blinks, surprised by this abrupt shift in the conversation—so far most of their talk has centered on work matters. "Yes, as a matter of fact. A daughter. In Chicago. She's a city planner."

"Is she married?"

Frowning, he taps the breadbasket with one hand, then bats it back with the other. "No, but she's seeing someone. I think he's married. He told her he's divorced, but . . ." He looks up, startled. "I don't know why I'm telling you this."

The information does strike her as unusually personal, opening an unexpected window through his dignified façade. His concern for his daughter makes him seem more real. But since he looks a bit uncomfortable, and because she's the expert in protocol, she changes the subject. "Would you like to hear a funny story?"

He nods.

"I heard about this restaurant from a neighbor of mine named Carol. She said that one Christmas she gave her mother a coffee table book about classic Roman art and architecture. It had a full-page photo of Michelangelo's David, but her mother cut out a pair of shorts from construction paper and pasted them over, you know, the appropriate place."

She shifts in her chair. *The appropriate place.* What a schoolmarmish phrase! She pictures naked David; reaches for her wine glass.

Charles grins.

Thankfully, the waiter appears with their salads. As Grace struggles to cut a recalcitrant cherry tomato, this dating strikes her as a fragile thing, like a boat easily rocked by an awkward comment or a too-personal revelation. What if she inadvertently says something that displeases him? And how has she reached a point where she cares so much?

"More wine?" Charles reaches forward with the bottle.

"Just a touch. Thank you." She looks up at him, at his thoughtful, courtly face, his rich ebony skin gleaming in the candlelight. In the Islands, people would have looked down on him for that. Light skin was better than dark. Non-kinky hair was "good" hair. According to these stereotypes, he looks too dark, too African. Ashamed of herself, she looks down at her plate. After a moment, she looks up at her date. He has a handsome face. And kind.

"Thank you for coming out to Brooklyn," she says.

He waves a hand dismissively.

"No, really. Many people from Manhattan never come out here, even though this neighborhood is just across the river. It's as if you were asking them to go to another state."

"It's my pleasure," he says; he looks earnestly across the table and she believes him. There are so many questions she wants to ask. *Why me? What happened with your wife? How will this evening end?*

Instead, they discuss the board meetings at the Beardon Group, joking about Mr. Laidlaw's habit of rushing the dinners because he'd rather be at home.

"Are there any other black executives in your office?" she asks.

He pauses for a moment. "There's one other vice-president. To tell you the truth, though"—he grins, almost in apology—"I don't like him much."

Emboldened by the wine, by their growing intimacy, she asks, "Do you ever feel lonely at work?"

He looks sad all of a sudden. "You know," he says wistfully, "down where I come from, we have a saying: In the South, black folks can get as close as they want to white folks, but just don't try to move high in their world. In the North, you can get as high as you want, as long as you don't get close."

That seems to sum things up. She looks frankly at him, and he returns the look. In all of her nervous thoughts about what might happen when two people come together, this is something she has overlooked: a chance to be understood.

"I hear some big changes may be underway at the Beardon Group soon," Charles says.

Suddenly shy, Grace looks down at her napkin. So far, she hasn't mentioned her dream of a promotion.

"You do an excellent job there," Charles continues. "Everyone speaks very highly of you."

"Thank you," is all she says. Over the years she has overseen a number of major events for the top executives, has filled in for the Director of Hospitality during some of his vacations. She has thought a lot about the matter and concluded that there isn't anyone at the Beardon Group who can come close to matching her qualifications for the job, but she doesn't want to jinx the possibility by talking about it.

As the waiter removes the remains of their salads, Charles clears his throat. "I'm having a very nice time tonight."

She flushes with pleasure. It occurs to her that this dating business may not be so easy for him, either—that it may have taken a good deal of courage for him to ask her out.

"I hope I didn't put you to too much trouble, that first time you asked me to dinner," she says, thinking of the CD he sent and of the calls he made to overcome her protests that she was too busy with work. He has been so patient and so unpressuring.

"I believe it was worth it," he says.

Her skin feels warm, glowing. Perhaps romance doesn't have to be so traumatic after all—perhaps it can be a gentle easing away from the shore.

* * *

There's an awkward lull after the dessert and coffee, while they wait for the waiter to bring the change. To get to the restaurant, Charles took a car service directly after work, but now there's the matter of how—and when—he'll get back to Manhattan. Until now, each of their dates has ended with a chaste kiss on the cheek, and taxis bearing them to their separate homes.

"It's no problem," he says. "I'll just take the subway."

"Oh, don't go through all that trouble. You can call a car service from my house," she says briskly, as if she has just made some tactical accommodation at work, as if her suggestion is not charged with a world of uncertainty and possibility.

"All right," he replies, equally businesslike. "That would be easier."

The waiter returns. As Charles goes off to get their coats, Grace slips into the ladies room. She takes a powder puff from her purse and smooths some perspiration from her face. Quickly chews an antacid.

She joins her date outside and together they stroll down Court Street, pausing to look in a store window or exclaim about the prices on a real estate agency's photos. They discuss the neighborhood, a film they've both wanted to see, a problem she's been having with her computer at work. Two-thirds of the way home she's seized by a moment of panic: what if their conversation dries up before they reach her house?

They manage to keep the ball in the air. "Almost home," she says with a dry mouth as they turn onto her side street. Even with the night so cold, a young Latino neighbor with a little tuft of beard sits out on his stoop, drinking a Heineken and watching them dispassionately as they walk past. As they approach her front gate, Grace reaches into her purse for her keys.

"Are you planning to go to the conference at the Marriott on Friday?" Charles says, but she can tell he's just asking to avoid silence. He flinches as the iron gate clangs shut behind them. Discovering that he too is nervous lessens her own tension. As the door swings open she performs a mental survey, trying to remember if she left any dirty dishes in the kitchen sink. She precedes Charles inside and reappraises her home.

"This is really very nice," he says, and she follows his gaze as he takes in the elegant pattern of the molding in the entryway, the polished wood of the banister leading upstairs to the bedroom, the dried flower arrangement on the hall table.

By day the kitchen looks airy and cheerful, but at night there's something hollow about the room, with its one dinner plate in the dish rack.

"Would you like some coffee or tea?" she asks. "I mean, I can call the car service in a minute. They come very quickly. Or maybe you'd like something stronger? I think I might have some Irish whiskey somewhere. It was a present." She turns away toward the cabinets over the sink, realizing that she's been blathering.

Charles still has his hands in the pockets of his tweed coat. "Maybe," he says, grinning now, "we could make coffee and put some of the whiskey in it."

"Oh," she says. "Why not? Would you like to take off your coat?"

He shrugs off the coat and she bustles out to hang it in the hall closet, wondering as she does so if this doesn't seem to imply a longish stay—perhaps she should have draped it casually over a chair?

She returns to find Charles standing by the kitchen table, trying to peer out into the dark yard.

"You can't see it very well," she says, "but that's my garden out there. My pride and joy."

"My ex-wife loved to garden," he says, then winces. They haven't discussed his ex-wife, except in passing. He turns to the window again. "It's hard to see out, with the reflection of the lights inside here."

"I can turn them off." She crosses to the doorway and clicks the switch. The kitchen drops into darkness, but the courtyard outside jumps into sharper relief. Even from the other side of the room, she can see the outlines of the yards, the plants catching a faint light from random windows in the court.

Shyly she steps forward to stand next to Charles. Above the yards and the jagged trees, several hard diamonds shiver in the night sky. To the left, two bright floodlights beam atop the towers of the projects. Across the way, Carol Fasone stands in her brightly lit kitchen, washing some dishes. It has been some time since Grace has seen Milosz out in the courtyard, and she has heard a rumor that they've had some trouble, but her friend hasn't told her anything directly.

"Do you get along with your neighbors?" Charles asks, ending a charged silence.

"Mostly," she replies, looking at Carol and thinking also of her casual contacts with the Marshalls, the Martinezes and the Bretts. But then there's Melba Wilson, who gives her haughty looks as she passes by, as if to say *Who do you think you are, dressing that way, speaking like that? You think you're fooling anybody?*

Silence descends again as they gaze out into the dark courtyard.

"Look," Grace says. Charles presses closer to the window and they watch as snow begins to fall, big lazy flakes rocking down out of the dark sky.

Charles clears his throat, standing there next to her, and then she feels his hand brush across her cheek. She turns, and he moves closer, and suddenly she passes from the outside to the inside of the world.

CHAPTER TWELVE

MUTHAFUCKA AT THE DOOR GONNA KNOCK YOU RIGHT DOWN. THE OLD song had it right, Jamel thinks, as he walks out of Modell's Sporting Goods and onto Fulton Street. He scrunches into the collar of his coat to keep out the hissing winter wind. It's the Previous Employment section on the job applications that gets him every time. How's he supposed to have Previous Employment if no one will give him a job in the first place?

He has already wasted a couple of days just walking around screwing up his courage. He goes out in the morning when most of the other kids he knows won't be here—he doesn't want them to see him dressed this way, thanks to his mother's intervention. (The first morning, she grabbed him on his way out of the house, turned him around, and marched him back inside. "Put a belt on, boy! Who you think is going to hire you if he sees your underwear hanging out like some kind of hoodlum? Take that hat off! You have to look *clean* if you want some boss to treat you right.")

To start, he looked around to see where other teenagers were working already. He thought he could at least get a job as a stock boy in a shoe store or a department store, but soon he noticed that even the most menial jobs were filled by workers in their twenties or older. Most of the streets stalls were manned by either Pakistanis or older black men. The only places with teenage workers seemed to be the fast food franchises, and those jobs looked too stupid to him. Wear some wack polyester outfit, flip burgers all day, make minimum wage—No, sir! Finally he bit the bullet and starting walking into stores to ask if there were any openings. He received his first application from The Wiz, with its damn Previous Employment line. The manager scanned his skimpy responses, shook his head, and said, "We'll call you if anything opens up." Jamel chewed his lip and continued on down Fulton Street. After almost a week, he's filled out twenty applications, but many of the businesses didn't even give him a form, as if they didn't want to waste the paper.

He plods along the mall, trying to figure out where to turn next. He thinks of Tree, in his sentinel job in front of the crack house. It may be fucked up, but at least it's a job. He tried to talk Tree into joining his own search, but his friend scoffed at the idea. "How'm I gonna get a job if I put down on the application, 'Address: Wysocki Houses'? Shee, I might as well go in wearin' some motherfuckin' prison clothes."

It's beginning to occur to Jamel that he might not find a job at all. Who knows, maybe even McDonalds would turn him down for lack of Previous Employment. He looks at his watch: only four o'clock, but already the sky is graying into night. There are still some places he hasn't tried down near Flatbush Avenue, but he feels too discouraged to check. He pulls his gloves out of his pockets and trudges home.

Inside the front hall, he's grateful for the silence: his mother must still be at work, so he is temporarily spared a quiz about his success or lack thereof. He slings his coat over the banister and tromps down to the basement, where he pops a Jay-Z CD into the boombox and sinks into the old beanbag chair. The Styrofoam beads inside squeak as he readjusts his weight. Then the music kicks in, bass bumping, rhythmic vocal soothing. He closes his eyes. After a few minutes, the music pulls him inside itself, clearing his mind of past frustrations and future worries. He soaks in it like a healing bath.

*　*　*

"To start, I can only give you three shifts a week, lunches, eleven a.m. to three."

Ricky the Manager sits behind the desk in his brown poly tie and beige short-sleeve shirt, filling in the bottom of Jamel's application. He's black, like most of his employees. A corkboard behind his head is plastered with pamphlets from the Board of Health and Department of Labor. The little office smells of fried grease and stale coffee, but not as bad as the kitchen and register line outside.

Jamel tries to pay attention while the man talks, but he can't help glancing anxiously through the glass wall at the crew scurrying around in their royal blue polyester shirts and visors, scooping up fries, wrapping burgers, pressing cups against the drink dispensers. Most of them are girls.

"Here's your time card," Ricky says. "Stick it in the clock outside my door and then leave it in the rack. Don't forget to punch out or you won't get paid."

"How much do I get?" Jamel mumbles.

"Well, of course we start you out on minimum wage, but if you put in enough time with us, you can work your way up to more hours, better pay, and even benefits. This is an excellent opportunity; I became a manager here after only two years." Jamel wonders how long it took him to learn to speak so white.

Ricky gets up and hands him a shirt and visor. "Try not to get these messed up, because you're responsible for taking them home and cleaning them." He pops a video into a combination TV/VCR. "Watch this, and then come out and find me."

Jamel perches on the edge of his chair as some bright cheery music swells out of the little TV. He only catches bits and pieces because he's too distracted. "For your own safety and the health of our customers, always make sure you wear plastic gloves when you are working at a food prep station!" chirps a smiling face. The clock on the office wall reads eleven fifty-eight; outside, the food preppers whirl around, slapping on condiments and bagging orders in a dizzying swirl of royal blue. "Operating a Fry-O-Lator is serious business," says a young manager onscreen. "Keep your eyes on your work and save conversation for your break!" Outside, beyond the cash registers, lines of lunch customers already stretch to the doors.

A chime sounds. The video goes blank. Jamel stands up as Ricky pops his head back in the door.

"I forgot to tell you. You get a free meal after your shift is over. You can have burgers and fries, but no specialty sandwiches or desserts."

* * *

For his first three shifts Jamel works the Fry-O-Lators. He rips open bags of frozen fries, dumps them into metal baskets, then presses buttons to make them descend into the bubbling oil. The baskets rise robotically and loud beepers sound. In the middle of the lunch rush the demand sends him hustling back and forth, dumping fries into the oil, rescuing them above the oil, trying to avoid splashing the oil on his polyester shirt, which has already soaked up a smell of grease that even repeated washing won't remove. He runs back into the freezer for more bags and returns to a cacophony of randomly staggered beeping. In the middle of this confusion, he hears a familiar voice and turns toward the registers, behind which stand Tee-Ali and a couple members of his Wysocki Houses crew.

"Yo, PeeWee! Where our fries at?" Tee-Ali stares at him through his dark shades and hoots. "You slow as a motherfucker—I'm'a have to complain to the manager."

Jamel doesn't even have time to react to these jibes: already his coworkers are sticking their heads around the corner to ask what's the slow-down. The girls seem to handle the job with great aplomb, but Jamel's blue shirt is soaked with sweat. He figured the job would be easy but boring—he never realized that it would be boring and *hard*.

* * *

After work, as he sits exhausted at one of the tables in the back and eats his measly little hamburger and fries, he figures some math on the back of a napkin. His mother has agreed to pay for a third of the sound system. If he gives half of his after-tax earnings to Shanice for their daughter and manages to save the rest without spending any of it on junk, then he should be able pick up the full system in . . . *damn*: almost a year.

Later, he sits in his basement listening to a Ludacris CD while Tree sits across from him preparing a blunt: with the tip of his tongue clamped between his teeth in concentration, his friend peels open a Phillies cigar, pulls out the inner tobacco, and dumps in a good quantity of pungent blue-green marijuana. Jamel's mother is upstairs, but he doesn't worry about that: they have a tacit agreement that if he stays at home, she won't pry into his affairs.

"I can't understand why you still down with that burger bullshit," says Tree. "I make more in half a hour than you make in a whole day and all I gotta do is stand there and listen to my Walkmans, while you running around like a chicken 'thout no head."

Jamel doesn't answer, just sullenly opens and closes the CD case.

Tree rolls the end of the blunt in his mouth to seal the tip and reaches across the table for his lighter. "It ain't just how much money you makin'—it's where the other money go."

Jamel looks up. "What you mean?"

"Check it out: over in BPW, you got a bunch'a black people makin' them burgers. Every customer' order wurf what you make in a hour, and they got thousands of customers in there every damn day. Almos' all that money go into them registers and get shipped off to some white moefuckee in some big house way out the city. Now, in *my* business, you got some white moefuckee drive up in his fancy car to buy a little somethin', he givin' his shit to the brothers, yo—the money comin' *in*. Tell me I'm wrong, but that shit makes more sense."

Jamel doesn't reply. He has the day off tomorrow, but already the thought of putting on his blue shirt and visor again fills him with dread. It would be a lot easier to take up some shifts on Tree's job, but he knows his mother would go crazy if she ever saw him on that stoop.

* * *

Back at work, Ricky offers to make the job easier: he switches Jamel to burger detail. Now he spends four hours feeding frozen hockey pucks into the broiler's conveyor belt. On the way home, stinking of grease and bored out of his mind, he passes a handwritten sign in the window of a big diner called Three Kings: *Dishwasher Wanted*. On impulse, he stops in and asks about the job. This time, he has Previous Employment. One minute later, he has a new job. Halfway home, he stops on the street, takes his blue polyester shirt and visor out of his knapsack, and stuffs them into a trashcan.

* * *

This time, he gets two day and two night shifts. The owner's a gaunt, elderly Greek man known to one and all as Mr. K. During the day, the place bustles with a lunch business made up of city workers and lawyers from the nearby courts. At night Mr. K., unwilling to go home to his wife, sits at the bar and orders shots of bourbon from Manny, the curly-haired, mustached bartender, while the jukebox plays Ray Charles's "Georgia" or the Mills Brothers' "Glowworm."

"Manny," Mr. K. calls out sadly several times an hour, "get me another drink, and make it a double." By the end of the night, the boss's head has sunk down to rest on his bony arms on top of the bar, and Manny and Jamel have to call a car and lead him to it to make sure he gets safely home.

Back in the kitchen, Jamel shares the day shifts with a scrawny, tattooed, perversely cheerful white ex-con named Dean James. Dean wears his gray hair slicked back and tied off with a red bandanna. Only five feet tall, he works harder than Jamel has ever seen anyone work in his life, hauling heaping bus pans over to the Hobart dish machine and stacking them in the racks like some kind of demon— except for the slow times, when he'll wipe his hands on his apron, flash a grin, tap Jamel on the shoulder, and say, "You know where I'm goin', don't you, Jarmel? I'm goin' to get my *hit*." And then he walks bowlegged back to the filthy employee bathroom, where he has stashed a six-pack of Colt 45 tallboys.

One of the worst parts of the job is the end of the night shifts, when Jamel has to wrest the heavy rubber mats off the floor, smelling of Clorox, decaying food, insect parts, and grease, and heave them up over the side of the metal sink to spray them down. Another bad part comes when he has to haul bags of trash out the back, carry them down a dark alley, and swing them up into a foul-smelling dumpster. Not infrequently, big rats flee from under it at his approach.

Why does he stick with this job and not the other one? The work here is tougher, his clothes more soaked with sweat at the end of the night—but at least they're his own clothes, not some wack monkey outfit. On his meal breaks, he can eat anything he wants except for steak and shrimp—the rest of the food is so mediocre they don't care what he orders. At the end of the night, Manny will even pour him a beer. The job is demented, spending nights hosing half-eaten Reuben sandwiches into the garbage disposal while, through the kitchen door, he hears Mr. K. crooning along with his drunken buddies to songs on the jukebox by some jive singer named Nana Mouskouri. Occasionally Jamel will overhear them telling some joke and the word "nigger" will jump out, but what's he going to do? Complain? Quit? At least he's not one of twenty faceless teenagers ordered to smile by some big company.

The work is crushingly physical, but there's a certain pride in standing sweat-soaked next to the dish machine at the end of the shift, knowing he has had the stubbornness and willpower to make it through. And there's a huge reward if he can stick with it, a great machine of his own, just waiting to deliver him a glorious, god-like thunder.

CHAPTER THIRTEEN

IN THE MORNING CAROL STARES OUT HER BEDROOM WINDOW: THE trees look upside down, as if their branches are roots that have been wrenched up and splayed against the gray sky. The severely pruned fig tree in the back of the Paladinos' yard, wrapped in plastic, leans into the wind like a crude statue. A light snowfall rests on the gardens like a dusting of confectioner's sugar, but the result is not sweet: the courtyard's clouds of summer green have been stripped to a stark white geometry.

Across the court, the windows of the houses stack in rows; they remind Carol of playing Concentration as a child. Turn over a card and try to remember the location of its mate. She plays this game almost every waking minute now, time shocked backwards as she sorts through each memory of her life with Milosz to puzzle over its hidden face.

Those nights in bed when she reached out for him but he rolled away—at the time she assumed that he was too saddened by the evening news to think of making love. Was he just recoiling from her touch? Their sex life together hadn't been all she might have wished but there had been moments of passion. How could he fake those, force himself to fake them? Technically speaking, it doesn't seem possible that a man could be so devious as to fake an erection. It was foolish of her to think she could bring this stranger into her life, this transplant that never wanted to take root.

So far she has had no word from him, and in a perverse way she's grateful, since this allows her to preserve some hope, to spin out more optimistic explanations for his disappearance. Perhaps he is just experiencing a temporary fear of commitment, or some sort of premature midlife crisis. In her wilder moments she can even imagine that he has gotten into trouble with the Eastern European Mafia and gone into hiding. She tries to imagine him in a hotel room, or more likely camped out on some friend's sofa, but no picture will emerge.

Dressed only in her nightgown, she steps quietly downstairs, hoping that her mother may have already left the house—it's terrible watching the old woman trying so hard not to gloat. The empty kitchen, facing north, is sunless at this early hour. Across the courtyard her friend Grace, dressed for work, opens her kitchen window, sticks her head out, and looks up toward the sky. No one goes into the court now—it has been left to the pigeons huddled on the phone wires, bellies puffed against the cold. How easy it would be to follow their example, to let her mind retreat from the cold world, to sink inward like a bird pressing its head into its own warm feathered breast. To sleep.

It's hope that holds her up on this chilly morning. It makes her hands tremble as she pours herself a cup of coffee; she must suppress her excitement in order to pick up the phone and dial the office.

"Amy, I'm sorry, I'm not gonna be able to make it in again today."

"Are you okay, hon? Maybe you should get a doctor to check you out—a week is a long time to be having stomach troubles."

"No, it's just a little flu, is all. Are you sure you're okay with covering my phone?"

"I'll manage," her coworker says. "Everybody's asking about you."

Carol knows what that means: Messieurs Burkett, Christiansen, and Chang are anxious to have her in the office again. Three grown men, and they can barely make a photocopy.

"Is Milosz taking care of you?"

"He's—I'm fine, really. I better let you get back to work. Say hi to everybody for me."

She hangs up, rubs her fingers over her grainy eyelids. She thinks about those first weeks after Milosz left, how she braved it through work each day, not letting the others know that anything was wrong. Her sick days are used up; now she's into her meager stock of personal days. What will she do when those are gone?

She goes up to her room and dresses quickly, then returns to the kitchen to lift her coat off the hook behind the door.

Her mother appears in the doorway, her sparse hair undone and sticking out from her head in a frizz of static.

"Carrie, aren't you going to be late for work?"

"I'm not going in today."

"Where are you going, then?"

"I'll be back soon."

"Please, honey," her mother says. "Don't go. It's not going to help anything." She moves into the room with a tender tragic look on her face and Carol is almost overcome with an urge to rush toward her, surrender, to collapse into her arms. She moves forward but rushes past, stifling a sob as she flees the house.

* * *

She walks the long way to the Polytechnic University, skirting the edge of the Fulton Mall—it makes her uneasy to walk there, to feel herself the minority in a sea of colored faces. The black people are so wrapped up in their own world, their coded way of talking; they hardly acknowledge her presence as she passes, as if they share some sort of tacit agreement that the best way to deal with a white woman in their midst is to pretend she isn't there. "Those people will not bother you," Milosz told her, in one swoop dismissing not only her feelings but the entire mix of blacks, Pakistanis, Koreans. . . . Perhaps it takes an extra five or ten minutes to walk around the edge, but it seems easier for all concerned.

And so, safely past the mall's congested heart, she turns up a side street, which leads her onto a plaza separating the Metrotech office complex from the boxy buildings of the technical college. A chill wind swirls through the square, sending the last scraps of fallen leaves skittering across the concrete. At any second Milosz might walk out of those big glass doors up ahead, joining the ranks of students striding purposefully across the square with knapsacks slung over their shoulders, these young Vietnamese and Arabs and West Indian students eager to learn the technical secrets of American success.

Carol steps across slush crystallized on the sidewalks like piles of broken safety glass, but she is warmed by her determination, her sense of purpose. She pulls her hat over her ears, brushes the snow off a bench facing the entrance doors, and settles down to wait.

If she doesn't see Milosz today, maybe the phone will ring soon. Maybe a letter will arrive. Tonight, even, he might return. If I can just talk to him, she thinks. I'll try not to shout. I can find it in my heart to forgive. Like a Christian. We can start over and forget this unfortunate episode, this stutter in our marriage.

The cold of the bench seeps into the back of her stockinged legs.

* * *

Two weeks later, she sits with some co-workers in the back booth of a restaurant on Ninth Avenue. Every Thursday the secretaries from Burkett, Christensen, & Chang take their lunch break at P.J. Henry's, this carryover from the eighties, with its hanging ferns, butcher block tables, and stained glass windows.

The group stares at a waiter weaving his way through the crowd.

"A *tush* from Heaven," sighs Amy, a plump young redhead who works for Mr. Chang. The food is just average here, but the sight of this waiter's taut little butt is an unadvertised special. "The only thing I like better than watching him walk toward me is watching him walk away," Amy adds, and the women chuckle.

There was a time, Carol remembers, when she'd have joined in with the merriment. Hell, there was a time when she'd have instigated it. But then Milosz left, and—inevitably—the word got out around the office, and recently she has endured an outpouring of consolation to her face, and a crackling of gossip behind her back, and the others have listened to her sad story so much that she has finally exhausted their stock of sympathy. What really tipped the balance seems to have been her refusal to take revenge.

"I know this was terrible," Amy said one day after lunch. "You must be still getting over the shock and all, but what are you going to do about it?"

"*Do?*" Carol replied. "What do you mean?"

"Honey, all you have to do is pick up the phone. Just because he has his green card doesn't mean those Immigration people are going to let somebody put one over on Uncle Sam. You make one call, and the next thing he knows, that asshole will be sitting on a plane headed right back to Yugoslavia or whatever the hell they're calling it these days."

Carol sat stricken, too shocked to even consider it. If this were some TV movie of the week, that would be the thing to do, get her revenge on the evil lying husband—but what if he wasn't evil, just confused?

The other women in the office agreed with Amy. "Teach that dog what you think of his tricks."

But I still love him, Carol wanted to shout. She knew that would sound stupid, so she kept her mouth shut.

After a few days, the others gave up arguing with her. Now she sits quietly at the edge of the booth while they enjoy their break.

"I don't know why," Amy is saying to Sheila, Mr. Christensen's secretary, "with my first I didn't have any problems, but when I was pregnant with Heather I broke out like crazy. I used to use a concealer, but it's so hard to find one that matches your skin tone, you know?"

Carol looks dully at her co-worker, at her lovely rosy skin. She looks down and she's eating some pasta primavera and she doesn't even remember the waiter bringing the food. She crunches into a broccoli floret and the blend of tastes—garlic, parmesan cheese, olive oil—anchors her back in the present. Now Amy is admiring Sheila's hair extensions. My God, Carol thinks, is this what we're like? After thirty years of women's lib we sit around on our lunch hour talking about hair and makeup and some waiter's butt?

"Hey, Fasone . . ."

A meaty hand thumps on her shoulder and she looks up to see Tom McGlynn from Accounting buttoning his overcoat.

"How do ya get a nun pregnant?" he says, an expectant smile lighting his broad face.

"Dress her up as an altar boy," she says, spoiling his fun, and she's seized by a sudden urge to weep.

"What's the matter with you?" McGlynn says, pulling his gloves out of a pocket. "You're so goddamn serious around the office—what happened to the life of the party?" A puzzled expression overtakes his smile and Carol looks across the table to intercept Amy's frantic wave.

"It's okay," she says, and turns back to McGlynn. "My husband left me."

McGlynn stands there, struck dumb. He actually blushes. "Jesus, Carol, I'm so sorry. I didn't know. If there's anything at all . . ." He winces and pulls on his hat. "See you gals back in the salt mines," he says, and slips away.

"It's okay," Carol repeats, in response to Amy's red face. She twirls some linguine around her fork. Amy turns to Sheila and starts in again with the makeup talk.

The life of the party. Carol turns the phrase over in her mind. Is that how McGlynn sees her? Maybe the others do, too. Funny Fasone from Mr. Burkett's office, who can be counted on to drink too many rum-and-Cokes at office parties and puff up her cheeks with her Lucille Ball impression. What a card. How did this happen, she wonders, how did this goofy office Fasone come to stand in for the dismal Carol Fasone who waited on the edge of disco dance floors watching her girlfriends get picked up?

She sets her fork down, uninterested in her congealing pasta, puzzling out this mystery: that everyone is not just one person, but the person they are at work, and another at home, and still another when somebody loves them.

One night, maybe two months after their wedding, she and Milosz had come home from a dinner at Michelangelo's restaurant on Court Street, full of chicken Marsala and tiramisu and glasses of sweet port.

Her mother was away that weekend, she can't remember why. Standing there in the kitchen, Milosz put his arms around her and crushed her to him, and with one broad sweep of his forearm he pushed aside the stacks of bills on the kitchen table and lifted her up and leaned her back and ran his fine-boned hands up her thighs. At first she couldn't help noticing a pencil rolling under her back, couldn't stop worrying about the bills disordered on the floor, about what Grace Howard might think if she should happen to stare out of her window at the dark kitchen across the way. But then Milosz was rolling down her panties, and pushing himself into her, and she was ready, so ready, and she let herself relax against the tabletop, let herself be made love to like—she realized with a sense of wonder—some character in a soap opera. *Swept away.* Milosz gripped her hips and pulled her toward him and suddenly she was coming, coming, convulsing and thrashing like never before. Her husband pulled out of her just before he came, and then he leaned forward and rested his warm torso on hers, and she inhaled his sweaty musk and clutched his damp, bony back. He whispered something into her ear.

"What?" she said, startled, even though she was pretty sure she had heard him the first time.

"You are the wild woman," he said again.

And then he pushed himself up and matter-of-factly tromped off down the hall to the bathroom, leaving her lying on the kitchen table with her panties around her ankles, amazed and exhilarated at this improbable new manifestation of Carol Fasone. *The Wild Woman*— who would ever have thought it?

CHAPTER FOURTEEN

"Hey, *Brett.*"

Mitchell turns away from a stack of paperwork to find his colleague Doug Parken leaning conspiratorially over the wall that separates their cubicles.

"What's up?"

"You wanna take a break?"

"Sorry; I have to get the reimbursements for all these vouchers out by five."

"Take a break," Parken says with an odd smile on his normally impassive, sallow face. "I got something to show you."

Mitchell looks at the vouchers, shrugs, and rises. Parken steps out of his cubicle carrying a small shopping bag.

"Where we going?" Mitchell asks, following. "To the kitchen?"

"No," Parken says. "In here." He veers off the corridor into a small private conference room, pulls Mitchell in, and locks the door. Through the window, smoke rises from a row of factory stacks across the East River.

"What's going on?"

Parken sets the bag down on the polished mahogany table. "I've been thinking you could use a little peace of mind."

Mitchell smiles uncertainly. "I thought we already did the Secret Santa thing at Christmas. What is it?"

Parken reaches into the bag, pulls out several wads of newspaper, then a bundle wrapped in a baby blue felt Mitchell recognizes from his mother's collection of Tiffany silver. Parken sets it on the table and peels back the cloth to reveal a sleek-looking pistol. "Peace of mind," he announces.

Mitchell looks up, confused. "They sell guns at Tiffany's?"

The question is so stupid that they both have to laugh.

"Go on," Parken says. "Pick it up."

Mitchell stares down in incomprehension. "Are you kidding? What am I gonna do with this?"

Parken leans forward. "Since you told me about the mugging, and especially that police line-up—that's pretty creepy stuff. I figured you could use a little protection."

Mitchell sputters. "This isn't some Charles Bronson movie. I can't just go walking around with a *gun*."

"Of course not. You don't want to carry it around—that'd be asking for trouble. I'm talking about a little home security."

Mitchell stares down at the blue-black weapon gleaming dully under the fluorescent lights. It smells of oil.

"Go ahead," Parken says. "Check it out."

Cautiously Mitchell reaches down and touches the grip.

Parken laughs. "The safety's on. It's not gonna bite ya."

Careful not to point it anywhere near his co-worker, Mitchell raises the weapon, surprised at how heavy it feels at the end of his arm. He sights along the barrel, but then quickly sets it down, trying to imagine how he might explain to Mr. Reincke how he accidentally blew out an office window. "I don't need this," he says.

"Yeah, well—if you're lucky, you won't. But it seems to me you already pushed your luck once. And besides, think of your wife."

"My wife?"

"That's right. Say you're lying in bed, and you hear somebody messing with the back window. One of your 'underprivileged' friends. You wanna protect her if he gets inside, don't you? Considering the firepower that's out on the street these days, he's liable to be coming at you with a Glock or a Mac-9, and you don't want to be standing there holding just your dick, am I right? This is a nice semi-auto."

"What does that mean?"

"Well, I'd give you the specs, but they wouldn't mean much to you. All you need to know is this: you gotta squeeze the trigger for every shot, but it reloads automatically from a ten-round mag. And it's got a nice light pull—you could get off eight or ten shots in a couple of seconds."

Mitchell wonders just how well he knows his colleague—this talk about shooting people is making him nervous. After a minute, though, Parken's forceful picture of the intruder starts to take shape in his mind. A big guy, coming through a window in the darkness . . . why not just say it? A black guy, from the projects. Carrying a knife . . .

Mitchell reaches out and hefts the pistol again.

"Look," Parken says, "chances are a million-to-one you're not gonna need this. You can put it up in your closet and then forget about it. The point is, you'll sleep better at night knowing it's there." He reaches back into the shopping bag and pulls out a clip. "If you need more bullets than this, I'd suggest moving out of that neighborhood tonight."

Mitchell sighs. "Well, maybe you're right. No harm in storing the thing. . . . How much would it cost?"

"Just give me a couple hundred," says Parken. "I got it in a package deal."

Mitchell hesitates.

"It's a lot cheaper than moving, bud."

Mitchell grimaces. "I guess so. Thanks."

"Don't mention it. Just one citizen helping out another. And don't get too picky about my latest petty cash voucher—I had a couple of dinners on there that were a little dicey." Parken picks up the gun. "Let's wrap this up so you can take it home." He reaches into the bag again and pulls out a couple of papers. "This is your permit application and a letter saying that I'm transferring ownership to you. It's all on the up-and-up. Just try not to pop anybody before the paperwork goes through."

* * *

Later, standing on the subway, Mitchell clutches his briefcase, which is heavy with his new purchase. How's he going to explain this to his wife? He resolves to just hide it when he gets home. Somewhere safe. Lord knows, there's no danger of the typical home handgun tragedy—the little kid climbing up and discovering the gun on a shelf. He looks around the car, wondering what the other weary F train riders would think if they knew what he was carrying. Some of them probably wouldn't bat an eye. Some of them are probably carrying guns right now—*packing*, as they say on the cop shows. He pictures some crazed gunman opening fire on the passengers, like that guy on the Long Island Railroad, then imagines himself as Charles Bronson, reaching into his briefcase and coolly blowing the guy away.

By the time the doors slide open at his stop, the fantasy has faded and he's anxious to get rid of the gun, to stow it away and forget about it.

In his front hallway, he calls out for Kristin. When she doesn't answer, he trots down to the basement and stashes the bundle in an old box, underneath his college yearbook and a couple of economics texts.

CHAPTER FIFTEEN

WHILE GRACE WAITS OUTSIDE THE BROOKLYN BOTANIC GARDEN for Carol, she sits on a bench in the shade. A steady flow of visitors presses through the turnstile, eager to take advantage of this first warm weekend at the end of an unusually cool April. The scene reminds Grace of a French painting, but she's not sure which one: Van Gogh's "Entrance to the Public Garden at Arles," perhaps. It wouldn't do any good to ask her neighbor—she remembers an afternoon years earlier when she suggested that they stop in to visit the Brooklyn Museum next door. Grace had been enthralled by a retrospective of paintings by Vuillard but—despite her friend's polite murmurs of enthusiasm—after half an hour she could sense that Carol was ready to leave. Later, her neighbor sheepishly confided that, in all her years of living in Brooklyn, she had never visited the museum.

"Gee, I'm sorry I'm so late."

Grace looks up to find her friend standing breathless before her.

"I was having an argument with my mother," Carol continues, "and I lost track of the time, and then the subway stalled for about ten minutes at Atlantic Avenue—"

"Please—don't worry about it. I was enjoying the weather." Grace stands and follows Carol through the entrance.

On the other side, Carol watches as her friend maneuvers through the turnstile, taking care to protect the creases of her pressed navy-blue skirt. Mentally, she shakes her head: here they've come for a weekend stroll in the park, and Grace is dressed as if for work or church. Doesn't she ever let her hair down and just relax? After all, it's *the weekend*—who's going to care what they look like?

It doesn't matter—the important thing is that Grace's invitation to go see the cherry blossoms has finally gotten Carol out of the house, after months of a dark inward spiral. In March, she had been coming home from shopping when she was struck by a sudden marrow-deep chill. That night she plunged into a fever that lasted for seven days—and seven nights of cold sweats, changing wet nightgowns, shivering uncontrollably, too cold to even get up and go to the bathroom. She was afraid; what if she spiked a high fever in the middle of the night and was too delirious to call for help? Her mother—her cantankerous, ornery mother—had really come through for her, making her chicken soup, washing the bedding, even staying on a cot in her room so she could monitor her temperature. At the moments when the fever loosened its grip, Carol couldn't concentrate enough to read a book, so she turned to her old standby, gardening catalogs. Even then, though, her bitter memories wouldn't leave her alone—they seeped in through the names. Alchemilla—*Lady's mantle*. Draconicum—*Leopard's bane*. Catananche—*Cupid's dart*. Dicentra—*Bleeding heart*.

Soon a distant rushing whisper of cars is the only sign that the two women are in the midst of a city. The sun high overhead casts short shadows as they wind along an asphalt path.

Grace breathes deep. It's good to be walking next to this lush, glossy lawn, to inhale the scent of these sweet purple lilac bushes standing in their beds of wood chips, to pass these trees breathy with young leaves. "Can we stop in here for a minute?" she asks as they come to the Rose Garden. She glances over, noting that her friend still seems pale, subdued, as if moving in her own private shadow.

"Sure," Carol answers. "I love this spot."

They pass under a trellis into a world of roses. Normally Carol likes to stoop down and read the little name plaques—*Valentine* beaming next to *Comtesse de Ceylon*, *The Prioress* leaning over toward

Escapade—but today she just stands in a walkway, staring into the distance, chewing her lip.

A rabbit darts across the walkway and Grace smiles. She looks forward to her own planting, sensing that—thanks to Charles Matthews—her garden will hold new meaning, that she has been brought closer to this world of growing things. She turns to Carol, thinking to share the news of her romance, but her neighbor looks so downcast that she holds back.

Carol turns; catching her neighbor's concerned look, she's tempted to unburden herself of her whole sad story, but the words have grown too bitter in her mouth.

They walk out under the trellis and head toward the Cherry Esplanade, turning first onto an avenue bordered by tall, noble trees—*Armistice Maples*, as a copper plaque says, *Planted November 11, 1918*. They step across a broad lawn, plush under their shoes, toward the evenly spaced clouds of pink blossoms, which are not as resplendent as usual, although this doesn't deter the Japanese families who stand in their shade, posing proudly for photographs.

"They must be late due to the cold weather," Grace says.

"Who?" replies Carol, looking up suddenly.

"The cherry trees."

"I'm sorry. I guess I'm a little preoccupied today."

Grace waits for a follow-up, which doesn't come. She walks on; her neighbor will say what's on her mind, or she won't. Either way, Grace will enjoy this perfect weather and this perfect place. She doesn't expect much in the way of personal confidences: for as long as they've known each other, their conversation has centered on such topics as the most efficient way to get rid of aphids, or how to nudge a reluctant begonia to bloom.

They cross a bridge over a little clattering stream, then stroll past an array of carefully tended bushes and shrubs, a medley of improvisations on the color green. At the eastern edge of the park, they come out onto a long plaza set around a pool filled with water lilies. Lazy orange fish are dimly visible through water so murky that it reminds Carol of the oil in a jar of sun-dried tomatoes.

A drop-legged heron suddenly flaps down out of the sky, snaps up a fish in its sharp beak, then perches on a lily pad to wrestle the fish into its gullet. The women turn to each other, astonished.

On the other side of the pond they push through a door into a dry, resin-scented greenhouse. Inside, the warm sun throws broad planes of light across the slate floor. The women meander around weathered pedestals topped by tiny Japanese maples, junipers, and pines.

Grace puts on her bifocals and tilts her head back to peer down at a plaque. "This tree is old as me!"

Carol pauses to read an informative display on the wall, which tells how the trees are kept small by regular pruning and pinching of the young shoots, how the trunks and branches are shaped by wrapping them with copper or aluminum wire, how a small pot restricts the spread of the roots. "The reaction of each person viewing the trees will be individual and personal," the sign concludes. "This is the uniqueness of bonsai."

With satisfaction Grace contemplates a Gingko Biloba rising from its mossy base, admiring the Asian sense of time which has shaped the little tree, the calm exercise of will and restraint.

Carol turns away from a Sargent Juniper, repelled by its stunted, gnarled trunk, its knotted branches that remind her of her mother's arthritic hands. She leaves the greenhouse and crosses toward a spray of tulips, their stems stirring in the breeze, blossoms cupping the light. The reddest reds, yellowest yellows. Normally, she would enjoy this burst of color, but today the display seems garish.

Grace moves out to join her. She prefers a subtler palette, but today the tulips match her mood.

The women move past the flowers, pausing to read the names. *Orange Emperor. Cheerleader. Dreaming Maid. Love Eternal.*

Grace, trailing along behind, sees Carol's shoulders jiggle and thinks she's laughing at one of the names. "What is it?" she asks, but her neighbor turns away. Grace realizes that she's silently weeping.

Carol sinks down onto a stone bench, sniffling as she opens her purse. She fumbles inside, but a gust of tears overtakes her and she blindly sets the purse down.

Grace reaches into her own purse and pulls out a packet of Kleenex. "What is it?" she says again, but Carol cannot answer.

Awkwardly Grace puts an arm around her friend's heaving back. "Here," she says, handing her a tissue. "It's all right, honey."

Carol buries her head against Grace's shoulder and sobs.

CHAPTER SIXTEEN

GRACE FEELS CHARLES'S SHOULDER MUSCLES BUNCHING UNDER HER hands, and he surges forward, again, again, and scoops his arms down beneath her back and hugs her so tight, pressing his face into her neck, and *Please* he moans and *God* and she feels his weight anchoring her to her bed, feels his chest meld into her own, one body together, and as he cries out her whole self is suffused with a pleasure so intense it doesn't seem possible, overpowering because it wells up from the same deep place as tears.

Charles lies for a moment with his weight on her, his chest a gasping bellows, and then he slides off to one side. Grace feels his hand touch her shoulder, as if to reassure her that he's still there. The covers have slipped to the floor; the air feels good on her overheated skin. She pulls the sheet up to cover her plumpish body, but feels foolish: his body is just as middle-aged, and after months together they don't have much left to hide. She sinks down onto the mattress, allows herself to relax.

Charles sighs contentedly. "Well, I guess there's some life left in the old man yet."

Though the room is dark she can picture his grin. She turns on her side and runs her hand across his furry chest, his domed belly; he's like a stout bear.

"You're a bear," she murmurs.

"Mmph," he says, and holds her hand up to interlace it with his own.

"Would you like some water?"

"No thanks—I'm okay. Better than okay."

She lifts her neck and slides a pillow under her head. She lies in a blissfully blank state until she feels a crick in her shoulder and shifts. Thoughts crowd back in.

"Charles?"

"Mm?"

"Do you mind if I ask—no, never mind."

"About my wife?" he says.

"Well . . ." He has spoken of his divorce a number of times, but for months they have skirted around any full discussion of his marriage.

"It's okay. But are you sure that this is the best time?"

She considers.

"I mean, if you want to talk about it, I'll talk about it."

She has noticed this about him, this effort to be open with her, to "communicate," as everybody says these days. She suspects that perhaps he was not so direct with his ex-wife, and he has had time to regret it. He asks questions, and listens when she speaks.

"No, that's all right." It's better to appreciate the moment. For now, she knows only what she has learned in casual conversation: that the wife kept the house up in Mount Vernon while Charles took an apartment near Columbus Circle; that his ex also likes to garden; that the last time they saw each other was at their daughter's college graduation. And she knows the most important thing: that though his voice is still tinged with sadness whenever he mentions his married days, he speaks of the divorce with finality. Let it go, she says to herself. The bluebird has landed on her shoulder—let it be. After all these years she has found love. If she gets her promotion, which will probably be announced very soon, she'll absolutely burst.

Next to her Charles's breathing slows, punctuated by an occasional snagging snore.

She grins. Her skin feels curiously buoyant these days. After almost thirty-five years, she realizes she has been wearing a stiffness to work like a business suit, restricting her face to a small palette of expression: a pleasant smile, a look of earnest inquiry, an accommodating nod.

She rolls over and looks at the clock. It's 12:30 in the morning and tomorrow is a workday, but sleep won't come. She still can't get used to the presence of another person in her bed. There are so many adjustments to make. They've started becoming a couple: doing things together, making plans, all of the things that so many people take for granted. She has learned that Charles has a characteristic way of pulling back his chin when he's not at ease, that he loves strawberry cheesecake, that he has a soft spot for sentimental movies and a surprising taste for modern art. Slowly they've learned about each other's past travels, and begun the unspoken process of mapping the most effective routes to each other's physical pleasure.

She wonders how she'll break the news to her married sister Amalie, who has grown so accustomed to her being a spinster, and she smiles as she contemplates telling her niece—college kids are not the only ones capable of having a little fun.

There's one person who will never get the news. What would her father make of all this? Technically, she's living in sin, having sex outside of wedlock, but surely that was a prohibition meant for young girls, rather than for women in their fifties. There was a time before her father became so stern, a time when her mother was alive, when he too must have experienced such easy, satisfying nights. A memory surfaces: her mother, in the living room, wearing a pink sheath dress and doing the Twist. She tries to remember where her father was at that moment. Standing on the sidelines, probably, grinning but too dignified to join in. And then her mother died, taking with her his last hopes for easy joy.

This is the risk, Grace thinks, her heart constricting. Giving up routine comforts, having to reorganize a living space—these are small sacrifices compared to the potential of so great a loss.

Through the window, green young sycamore leaves shimmer under a streetlight.

She reaches out in the dark and lays her hand on Charles's warm side.

CHAPTER SEVENTEEN

JAMEL IS HALFWAY OUT THE FRONT DOOR WHEN HIS MOTHER CALLS him back.

"Where you goin'?"

He holds up a black plastic bag. "Video store." He moves to push the door open again.

"How's your friend Tree these days?" she asks with studied casualness.

Wary, he stops short. *My* friend Tree? Tree, who practically grew up in this house, who is almost a member of the family?

Before he can put together an innocuous answer, his mother adds, "What's he doin' hangin' out in front of that house all day long?"

"You been listening to Marie again?" he parries. Marie is his mother's busybody friend, the neighborhood gossip, who happens to live several doors down from the house where Tree has been keeping his sentinel duty.

His mother plants her hands on her hips. "I don't need Marie to tell me what my own eyes can see, plain as day."

"He's not doin' nothin', Momma."

"Well all right," his mother says, "but if I ever catch you doin' what he's 'not doin',' you'll never leave this house again. You hear me?"

He winces, torn by loyalty to his friend, fear for his friend, love of his mother, fear of her. Is she ready to write Tree off in the hope that he won't contaminate her son?

"Jamel?"

He tugs his goatee anxiously.

"Come here," his mother orders. Head down, he complies. Instead of showing her wrath, his mother envelops him in a hug.

"You know why I'm telling you these things, don't you, baby?"

He squirms in the embrace, but his mother hugs him closer.

"I worry about you. I don't want you ending up like these other children. The House of Detention is no place for my son. If it seems like I'm hard on you sometimes, it's because I love you." Abruptly, she turns cheerful. "Now go bring back your video. Say hi to Onica for me."

Jamel nods and rushes out the door. On the sidewalk, he pauses to breathe deeply of the fresh spring air and to blink, trying to clear his heart of the weight of his mother. The gate clangs shut behind.

* * *

"*So*," says Onica, pointing at the Knicks watch cap peaking high above his head, "you supposed to be Sneezy or Dopey?"

Jamel grins despite himself. He slings the bag onto the counter and reaches for his wallet.

Onica looks over her shoulder. "Don't worry 'bout it." She reaches out a long orange fingernail and taps at the computer keyboard. "This video was never checked out, awright?"

"Thanks, Onnie." He notices a flashy new ring on her finger. "Is that real plastic?"

She makes a face. "Ooh, you so *funny*." She holds the ring up, the better to admire it. "Din't Tree tell you? We're *engaged*. This is real gold, real diamond—Tree don't buy me nothin' cheap."

The engagement doesn't come as much of a surprise—the pair have been planning to get married ever since seventh grade—but Jamel is hurt that his friend didn't confide in him. He doesn't see much of Tree these days. And the ring—this is no trinket bought at a stand in the Fulton Mall. It must have cost a fortune. He thinks of Tree, easygoing Tree, standing outside the drug dealer's house while edgy addicts slink past. Tree should be . . . where? Where else would he earn enough money for a real engagement ring?

Jamel bites his lower lip. "Don't you kinda . . . I don't know, don't you worry about him sometime?"

Onica turns away to stack a couple returned rentals. "He gonna be fine," she says, not looking entirely convinced. "He ain't carryin' nothin'. He ain't sellin' nothin'. They can't arrest nobody for standin' around. Besides, he just gonna do it long enough to make money for the wedding, get us started with a 'partment so we don't have to live wif my stepmuvver."

"Couldn't he get a more, like, a regular kind of job?"

"Doin' what? Burger King? You know how much I'm makin' here, Jamel? Minimum wage. On'y three shifts a week. Even if we was both workin', you think we could support a baby on a couple hundred dollars a week?"

Jamel clams up, silenced by the talk of supporting a baby. He's kicking in some child support money now, but not enough to be much help. He's just lucky his mother has a good job. He's lucky. Who is he to give somebody else advice?

"Bootie," Onica murmurs.

"Huh?" Preoccupied, he has no idea what she's talking about, but then a customer nervously slides the box for a Triple-X DVD across the counter.

* * *

Jamel dawdles on his way out of the store. He glances back at Onica and wishes she wasn't there today. If that new guy was working, the one who doesn't know him, he might have had the nerve to rent a sex DVD. Not one of the hard-core pornos—recently he saw one at a friend's house and it was sort of creepy: too-close closeups of sex organs pounding away like hairy industrial equipment. No, not that kind, but a couple of weeks ago he rented one of the Playboy DVDs and snuck it home when his mother was out. It was sexy but safer, those airbrushed, improbably big-breasted women staring dreamily up at him—there was even a black model.

By the time he leaves Video Magic the sun has already gone down, but way to the east, where the street rises toward Park Slope, an apartment window catches the last daylight, a tiny rectangle of molten gold. The evening is growing cool, but he's too restless to return home, so he wanders down Smith Street toward Atlantic Avenue. At Bergen Street, young white businesspeople swarm out of the subway and stride home purposefully, or stop in at the Korean deli on the corner to buy strange things like soy milk or low-fat cookies.

Up Atlantic stands the Williamsburg Savings Bank, tallest building in Brooklyn, the red neon hands of its clock tower branding the time on the settling dusk. Across the avenue, sodium vapor lights cast a yellow-green glow over the House of Detention.

* * *

At the end of a shift at the Three Kings, he's stacking clean plates on the shelves.

His colleague Dean James soaks a handful of bar rags in a bucket of bleach. "Hey, Jarmel," he says—he refuses to give up this pronunciation—"I'm gonna step outsahd and smoke me a Mar'bro."

Jamel shrugs and stands on tiptoe to return a couple of ramekins to the top shelf. Dean wipes his hands on his soggy apron and pushes through the kitchen door.

A moment later, Jamel hears some kind of commotion out in the dining room: muffled shouts, a yelp, the sound of furniture scraping on the floor. The noise grows louder until suddenly the door bangs open, revealing Dean crawling across the floor covering his head while a mountainous white guy in a red plaid jacket towers over him, kicking him and bellowing. "Get back in there, you little bastard!"

"Whud I do? Whud I do?" whimpers Dean.

It takes Manny the bartender, an unidentified customer, and Mr. K. (roused for once from his bar stool) to pull the big man off. "C'mon, Junior," says Manny, walking him out into the dining room and trying to calm him down.

Damn, Jamel says to himself. *If that's Junior, I'd hate to see Senior.* "What happen, Dean?"

His co-worker pulls himself forward across the floor and leans back against the dish machine. He holds a towel to his head to staunch a cut; with his other hand he reaches into his apron pocket. He sticks a cigarette in his mouth, but he's shaking too hard to light it.

"I don't know, kid—I just went out for some air, and that big ol' fucker was havin' an argument with his wife or somethin'. I guess he took it out on me."

"You ah'ight?" Jamel asks, bending down.

"I guess, but I'll tell you one thing for shore: I ain't never comin' back to this shithole. Will you do me a favor, Jarmel?"

"What?"

"Tomorrow night, I'm'a wait in that bar 'cross the street. You bring me mah check?"

Jamel nods.

* * *

Dean James finds work elsewhere. The boss decides not to replace him.

"You're a good worker," he tells Jamel. "You can handle it."

"But Mr. K.—"

"Don't sweat it, my friend. I give you an extra dollar an hour."

Jamel shakes his head, but doesn't argue.

By eleven o'clock the next night he feels like he has been run through the dish machine himself. He changes his clothes in the stinking employee bathroom, gets Manny to sign his time card, and finally steps outside, where the fresh air makes him feel like a man released from prison.

* * *

Two rough shifts later, he decides that Tree may be right: he's a fool to be slaving away when he could be making good money just standing on a stoop.

After work, he resolves to go talk to his friend about getting hooked up with some lookout work. His step lightens the farther he gets from the Three Kings. Two blocks from home, he almost bumps into Onica walking around a corner. She's moaning, as if in pain.

"Onnie, what's the matter? What happen?"

She raises a stricken face. "It's Tree, Jamel. They took him."

"Who did? Took him where?"

Onica sobs. "I told him I din't need no ring. I told him it was gonna be trouble."

Jamel grabs her by the arms. "What happened? Tell me what's going on."

It takes a few minutes for the story, punctuated by snuffling and sobs, to emerge. Tree has been caught up in a narcotics sweep, slammed against a fence, arrested, cuffed and taken away by the police. His court-appointed lawyer says that there's a real risk of a conviction.

* * *

At home, Jamel's mother takes one look at Jamel's face and makes him sit down in the kitchen. Too worried to put up a cool front anymore, he answers her questions truthfully; the whole story comes tumbling out, starting with the bizarre attack on his co-worker at the restaurant.

* * *

The next day, his mother announces that she'll pay the rest of the money for his sound system if he'll agree to stay out of trouble, at home.

CHAPTER EIGHTEEN

MITCHELL LIES NAKED UNDER HIS WIFE, REACHING UP TO HOLD HER hips. Not worrying about birth control has spiced up their sex life this past year, introduced a welcome element of spontaneity: they've been free to make love in the shower and even—once—standing in the garden shed. But there are times when he's struck by mortal dread; begetting a child seems like acknowledging that his race is run.

Recently, though, he has begun to see a brighter possibility. Maybe having a child will mean that he's not doomed to be an observer of life passing him by, not a victim of muggers or his father's mistakes or anything else. If he starts a family, maybe he can start everything over. Maybe he and his wife will get along better. As soon as he can save up some money he'll get out of the rat race and sign up for culinary school.

Right now, though, his body is flush with pleasure and he isn't thinking about anything except trying to hold back for another minute.

* * *

Two doors down, Grace sits in a sun-drenched corner of her garden, drinking a cup of tea and reading the Sunday *Times*.

Every few minutes she rests the paper on her lap, looks up, and basks in the heat. Although the fine weather has brought neighbors out into the courtyard, the leaves are restoring a sense of privacy to the heart of the block. Lavender morning glories flow toward her

along the fence. Farther down, crocuses spray up along the border of the flagstone walkway. Occasionally, off in the distance, she
glimpses a fellow gardener, a flash of color through the intervening
billows of green.

In subtle ways the gardens mark the passage of time. In the Paladinos' yard, new leaves rise out of the unwrapped fig tree's drastically
pruned branches, proof it has survived another Brooklyn winter. The
Bretts' shiny new chain-link fence has begun to rust. Every year the
trees in the court stand taller, blocking more of the sun, and the shade
creeps across the lawns a little earlier in the day.

Grace crosses the lawn to examine her peonies. The unopened
buds, like green candy jawbreakers, are studded with ants. She was
concerned that the bugs might kill the flowers but a recent gardening
column assured her there was a good symbiotic relationship at work:
in exchange for the rich nectar secreted by the leaves, the ants protect
the flowers from pests.

* * *

As Carol turns down her street, she's thinking about what happened
just an hour ago, as she was leaving work. She had turned off her
computer and was changing into her sneakers when Tom McGlynn
from Accounting leaned over the wall of her cubicle.

"Did you hear the one about the rabbi, the pope, and Al Sharp-
ton?"

Carol groaned. "What, do you have a brain tumor or something?
You told me that one last week."

"Oh," McGlynn's face fell.

Carol smiled to soften his disappointment. "Aren't you going home
now?"

McGlynn just fiddled with a little plastic troll sitting on the edge of
her desk; he stroked its bright pink hair. "I used to have one of these
when I was a kid."

"Really? I would've figured you for a G.I. Joe. Or the Joker, maybe,
from Batman." She bent down to slide her work shoes under the desk.

"Hey, Carol?"

She straightened up to find McGlynn looking at her with an uncharacteristically serious expression. "Yeah?"

He tugged at his shirt collar. "I wanted to tell you, I'm real sorry about what happened with your husband."

"Don't worry about it." Carol turned away to look for her keys. She expected McGlynn to drift off on his usual aimless rounds, but he stayed planted.

"Hey, Carol? Are you guys getting divorced? I mean, are you separated now, or what?"

She looked up sharply. "Why do you ask?"

McGlynn looked sheepish. "I dunno, I was just, uh, you know, wondering if you might wanna see a movie sometime, or something . . ."

Carol abandoned her search for her keys. "Are you asking me out?"

"Uh, I guess. I mean, I can understand if it's too soon, or something. You know—I'd understand, and all."

Carol could feel herself turning red. "That's really sweet of you, Tom, but—"

"It's too soon?"

"I don't know. I'm just surprised is all."

"You wanna think about it?"

In other circumstances, she *would* have thought about it. Despite McGlynn's corny sense of humor, he seemed to have a kind heart. And he was not bad looking, really. But it seemed inconceivable to go out on a date before she was absolutely sure her marriage was over. "I don't . . . I'm not . . . I mean—"

"It's too soon," McGlynn said. "I understand." He turned away, but then stopped. "Hey, Carol?"

"Yeah?"

"Let me know if you ever change your mind."

* * *

Down in his basement, Jamel Wilson gives out a deep groan of frustration.

"Why nothin' happnin'?" asks Shanice.

Jamel ignores her, tells her brother Darryl, "Push up the knob that say Master."

They're crowded around the mixing board of Jamel's new sound system. Darryl pushes the master fader but still all they hear is the faint buzz of the fluorescent lights.

"Why nothin' happnin'?" says Shanice.

Jamel tells her to shut up.

"*Yo*," says Darryl. "Don't be tellin' my sister to shut up."

"Piece of shit!" Jamel mutters, slamming his fist down on the table bearing the mixer and the 400-watt power amp. He can't believe it: after waiting so patiently for so long, after all he's been through to reach this special moment, the damned system doesn't even work.

Once again, he follows the power cord to the wall socket and makes sure it's firmly plugged in. He retraces the cables leading to the speakers: two big felt-covered, metal-grilled cabinets perched on chairs near the back door (for when they want to listen to music out in the yard), another two leaning against the wall by the storm cellar door (for listening on the front stoop). All of the connections look good.

"Let's go find that little Chinese bastard who sole it to you," says Darryl.

"What's this little button here?" Shanice says, reaching out toward the back of the amp.

* * *

In Grace's garden, the air fills with a shiny hissing, a sound like knives being sharpened, which is abruptly undercut by a hammering rumble. Shocked, she stares out across the yards.

* * *

Carol sits in her kitchen, wondering if she should have turned down Tom McGlynn's invitation. Suddenly the windows buzz, and through the wall comes a muted subterranean pounding. Her first thought is of another terrorist attack.

* * *

Mitchell's wife has just pushed him back against the pillows, smiling wickedly as she says "Don't move," when suddenly there's this incredible deep booming noise from outside. Mitchell's first thought—quite irrational—is that the Fourth of July has come early this year. After a moment, he realizes it can't be fireworks; the booms are too regular and closely spaced.

"Hold on a sec." He eases out from under his wife, stands and grabs his shirt from the floor to cover his crotch. The sound seems to be stronger in the rear of the house, so he tramps to the back and peers out the window. Down in the yard next door their West Indian neighbor, looking stunned, stares out over her fence.

* * *

The basement floods with 110 decibels of DXZ Crew. There it is, with stunning presence: first the sheen of the hi-hat; then the crisp crack of the snare drum; next the kick drum thudding so deep Jamel can feel it in his stomach; the fat loping bass line; a high persistent horn sample cutting through the low end rumble. Above it all, the rappers shout in unison, *Gimme da gat! Gimme da Gat!*

Jamel looks around at his friends, their faces open in rapture.

"Yo, this shit is *phat!*" he shouts with glee, his voice lost in the roar of sound.

* * *

The sound travels through the warm air of the courtyard, but also through the connected walls of the houses, through ceilings and floors, brick and beams, thudding into the very marrow of each neighbor's bones.

It's like a pile driver, a mining operation, a thundercloud.

CHAPTER NINETEEN

A WEEK LATER, ON HIS WAY HOME FROM WORK, MITCHELL COMES up out of the subway pulling off his tie. He rubs the back of his neck, already filmed with sweat though he has only been out of the air-conditioned train for a moment, but the swampy heat doesn't interfere with his good mood.

As he turns the corner onto his street, he walks past a group of black neighbors gathered on a stoop. They avoid eye contact or any greeting, except for a tiny boy thwacking a Hula-Hoop around his hips, who actually smiles at him. There's no need for this hostility, Mitchell wants to say. Maybe you're pissed off at white people, but you don't know *me*.

Halfway down the block he hears a burst of salsa music. Across the street lives a Hispanic family that spends nearly every waking minute out on their stoop. The patriarch is the young man with the tuft of beard under his chin who watched him get mugged that night last fall. The family members sit right next to each other on the stone steps, but they seem incapable of saying anything in a conversational tone: any dialogue, whether prompted by anger or good cheer, gets shouted across the intervening couple of feet.

Mitchell can't remember ever hearing his own mother raise her voice: she conveyed pleasure and displeasure alike in the same steely, restrained tone. His father would shout, yes, but only in rare moments of extreme anger that seemed to shock the very air of the apartment, that sealed, vault-like expanse. Anyone in the building who entertained too often or too loud would receive a letter on elegant stationery from the co-op board, and then they'd desist. No one would have thought of hanging out on the street, of eating food in public, of raising his voice above a murmured greeting. Mitchell doesn't look back on his old neighborhood with nostalgia, though—sometimes he thought he would suffocate in that so-clean, so-quiet world.

He pauses on his own stoop to sneeze. It's one of life's ironies: the sunniest days seem to be the ones that bring on hay fever. At least the house two doors down seems quiet. He hopes his neighbor won't be playing his damned new sound system this evening. Twice already Mitchell has called across the yards to ask the kid to turn it down. The teenager, looking a bit sheepish, complied, but after a few minutes the volume crept up again.

He sets his briefcase on a side table in the hall, throws his jacket over the banister, and goes into the kitchen for a beer. Through the open window he sees Kristin out in the garden. Like an angular saint kneeling in the midst of her flowerbeds, she stares blindly out across the yards. He sips his beer, not wanting to interrupt her reverie. What does she daydream about?

Perhaps, if he did ever go to a therapist, the good doctor could explain why he had traded one enigmatic woman for another. His mother had been a quiet person, but she carried herself with an air of sophistication and mystery; in her makeup, scarves, and big sunglasses she reminded him of Jackie O. After his father's downfall she had withdrawn further. Not because of the scandal—plenty of women in her circle had weathered all sorts of personal "difficulties"—but because of the family's subsequent loss of money and prestige. Home from college one Thanksgiving break, he had been sitting in a coffee shop when he spotted her gliding across Madison Avenue. She was without her sunglasses that day and her face looked like a Greek mask, rigid with makeup, her deep-set eyes shocking portals to the fear behind.

He dismisses these thoughts, determined to preserve his good temper. As he walks out into the yard hefting a bag of charcoal, Kristin turns, smiles, and wipes her forehead with the back of a soil-stained hand.

"Time to get that grill smoking," Mitchell says. He drops into a folding chair, kicks off his shoes, and hands the beer to Kristin, who takes a long pull.

"How was work?"

"Well," he says, pausing to take back the bottle and drain the beer, "I've got good news and bad. Which do you want first?"

She chews her lip. "The bad, I guess."

"The bad news is that we might have to postpone our vacation this summer."

She rocks back on her heels and frowns. "Why?"

He smiles. "Because of the good news: we met with Reincke today and he's very psyched about the second-quarter earnings. He said that if we can beat last year's third quarter by ten percent, the whole floor's gonna get a major bonus at Christmas. And that's not all." He leans forward with a big grin. "After the meeting, he took me aside and said in this real offhand way that soon he'll have to look into moving me into a real office."

Kristin squints up at him. "That sounds pretty vague. Does it count as a promise?"

He settles back happily. "I talked to Doug Parken about it this afternoon, and he said the man would never say anything like that unless some kind of promotion was being considered. The downside is that I'll have to really bust my ass this summer. But then in the fall, we could go to Italy like you always wanted, or take a house on Martha's Vineyard for a week. Something nice." He doesn't mention the best part: the promotion would enable him to save up enough for culinary school.

Kristin considers the news. "I guess that sounds pretty good."

Mitchell grins—he feels more confident than he has in years. "Good? This could be *great*. And one way or another, we're gonna have a kid. Or two. You'll see."

His wife looks up, surprised by his new morale.

"Listen," he says, "I'll be back in a minute. I'm gonna jog over to the market and get a couple of steaks. Why don't you get the coals going?"

* * *

Twenty minutes later he passes through the shed into the yard, this time bearing a shopping bag full of steaks, fresh corn, another six-pack, and some chips. The phrase *bringing home the bacon* occurs to him, and he grins. In an earlier age he would have come home with a freshly killed animal slung over his shoulder; now he pulls a couple of plastic-wrapped steaks out of a Styrofoam tray. But hey, isn't it the same thing? The man brings it home and then he sits back and enjoys his plot of turf.

He picks up a can of lighter fluid and squirts some on his new grill, brushing aside a childish fear that the coals will ignite the stream of fluid and the can will explode in his hand. Then he sits in the shade by the picnic table, munching a Dorito and watching his wife, framed in the kitchen window.

It hasn't rained for almost two weeks now and the air is quivering with heat. Next to the table a cloud of gnats fizzes over the stagnant water in a ceramic birdbath. He peers in at the green sludge of algae on the bottom. A closer look reveals some kind of microorganisms swimming about in the broth like tiny corkscrewing Sea Monkeys.

Two yards down, the back door opens and the black kid comes out, glances up at the sky, then ducks back inside.

Mitchell sips his beer and tilts his head back, looking up into the cool filtered light of the leaves. The yard is quiet, save for the occasional distant roar of a passing jet or some hidden insect making a high pipping noise like an old rotary phone.

And then: *Thoomp-Pop! Thoomp-thoomp-Pop!*

Mitchell winces at the barrage of sound. This time, the kid isn't even out back. What's the point of broadcasting to an empty yard?

Kristin comes out bearing a tray of plates and silverware. Mitchell looks over the fence and groans.

"Goddamned punk," he says. "What does he think—that he's the only person on the planet?"

"Just ignore it," Kristin says as she sets the table.

"*Ignore* it? How could I? It sounds like we're living next to a god-damned auto assembly line."

"Why do you let it bother you so much? He'll probably stop soon." Kristin bears the assault with a detachment that somehow drives his temperature even higher.

"Look, I've already asked him—politely—to turn it down. Several times. What do I have to do to get the message across?"

He rips the plastic off the steaks. Grimacing at the blood on his hands, he wipes them against the side of the picnic table. It occurs to him how blithely he has just been thinking about having kids and taking on new financial responsibilities. What if he doesn't get the promotion? What if he's stuck here listening to this kid blasting his gangster rap for the next few years? The music thumps and cracks across the courtyard. It's hard to make out the lyrics since the slang is so dense, but "motherfuckin' niggahs" seems to be a recurring phrase. Is this what the civil rights movement achieved: the opportunity for black people to denigrate themselves?

The steaks hiss as he slaps them on the grill. He sits and watches the gnats swirling over the birdbath like dizzy electrons.

After a minute he stands up. "I'm gonna go over there and talk to the kid."

"Let it go," Kristin says.

"Why? I'm gonna be calm and reasonable, but we paid good money to live here and we have a right to some peace and quiet."

* * *

He pushes open the gate in front of the kid's house. The front door is closed but the storm doors to the cellar are flapped open. The music is overwhelming now—he can hear not only the thudding bass but each distinct clash of cymbals, each angry word. Down through the low opening he sees the edge of a dress and some flip-flop-clad feet. He bends at the waist to make out the figure of the boy's mother sitting in the dim basement light. He's amazed that she would tolerate such a racket.

"Excuse me," he calls tentatively, but the music is so loud she doesn't hear.

"*Excuse me*," he shouts, and this time she turns and peers up. She swivels back to shout something into the interior of the basement.

The music stops.

The woman stands and climbs the stairs, emerging from the basement with a suspicious look on her broad face. She wears Bermuda shorts and a white polo shirt over her big hunch-shouldered frame.

"Yes?" she says, as if addressing some annoying salesman.

"I'm sorry to bother you," Mitchell says, feeling instantly foolish for the way he's opened the conversation—*him* bothering *her*. "I live just down the way," he continues, pointing at his house. "It's about the music. I've talked to your son several—"

"I don't know nothing about that. You'd have to talk to the owner of the equipment, and he ain't home right now."

Mitchell pauses, taken aback by this strange disclaimer. First of all, the woman certainly *does* know something about it, since she's sitting right next to where the stereo must be, and second, it hasn't been more than three minutes since he has seen her son in the yard. But calling her a liar isn't going to get him anywhere. The thing to do is to remain calm.

"Listen," he says in a reasonable tone, "I know that teenagers like to enjoy their music, but—"

"We own this property."

"Yes, I understand that, but my wife and I are just looking for a little peace and quiet when we—"

Fixing him with a baleful eye, the woman cuts him short. "We can do what we want on our own property. Now I don't have time to be standing out here like this." She turns away.

"Look," Mitchell says, struggling to keep his exasperation from showing, "I just want to talk to you as one human being to another . . ."

The boy's mother wheels around. "*You* look: this ain't no Greenwich, Connecticut. You livin' next to the Wysocki Houses now. My Jamel ain't hurtin' nobody. You want your peace and quiet, go buy a five-bedroom somewheres, and leave working people alone!" She snorts and descends sideways down the basement stairs.

Mitchell stands there for a moment, amazed by the abrupt end to the conversation. For the past week he has been trying to figure out why a mother would let her child get away with such aggressive behavior—now it occurs to him that she may actually be encouraging it.

The music comes thundering up again, louder than before.

His astonishment turns to rage. He's tempted to march down into the kid's basement and shut the music off himself. Why should he be afraid of a sixteen-year old? He reconsiders. Who knows who else may be sitting down there? This is New York: it would be stupid to get stabbed or shot over such a trivial matter. No—this is a civilized society and there are better ways to handle the problem: he'll call the police and let them deal with it.

* * *

He returns to his house and looks up the precinct in the phone book.

A bored-sounding woman takes his call. "Thank you for the information, sir—we'll try to send a car over as soon as possible."

"I'd very much appreciate that," he says, thinking, *Now* we'll put a stop to this nonsense.

He stands by the front window of the house, fully expecting a squad car to pull up, siren wailing, any second.

After ten minutes—no car—he suddenly remembers the steaks on the grill and runs down to his backyard.

"It's okay," Kristin says. "I turned them over and took them off. So how'd it go?"

He stares across the yard and scratches his jaw. "Not good. His mother told me that this isn't Connecticut. I decided not to mess around anymore, so I called the police."

"*Uh oh,*" Kristin says.

"Uh oh what?"

"I don't know if you want to stir them up."

"'Stir them up'? *I'm* the one who's 'stirred up'! They didn't leave me any choice. And now the goddamned cops won't even show."

The music slams across the yards.

"It can't have been more than a couple of minutes since you called," Kristin says. "Anyhow, this is Friday evening in New York City; I'm sure the police have more serious things to worry about than some kid playing his stereo too loud."

The gnats whirl crazily over the birdbath. Mitchell groans and sinks down onto the picnic bench. Suddenly the music stops, leaving a vacuum of silence in the courtyard. He hurries inside, trots across the first floor, and peers out over the front curtains, certain that he'll see a squad car in the street.

There's nobody out there except a little kid banging a broken hockey stick against the curb.

CHAPTER TWENTY

FROM A SHELF IN THE BACK SHED CAROL PICKS UP A TROWEL, SOME pruning shears, and her old leather gloves. Then she steps out into the yard to take stock. The early heat wave has browned the grass, but weeds are still sprouting in the flowerbeds, and some curling grape vines are sneaking over the fence from the McEvoy's house next door. From the back corner of the garden she peeks into the Brett's yard: Kristin has been over-watering the little succulent fingers of her *portulacas*.

She turns on the spigot for the hose, sets the spray for a fine mist, and gives her lawn a drink. A rainbow appears in the lustrous veil. She contemplates planting some scaevola along the borders of the sunken walkway: the little purple flowers will grow fast and bloom all summer, flowing over the stark concrete curbs. She thinks about a much more important plan: soon misters Burke, Christensen, and Chang will all be out of the office for a week and she'll be able to take some time off. Enough to finally track down Milosz.

Her mother steps out of the shed holding two glasses. "I brought you some iced tea," she says.

"Thank you, momma."

"It's good to see you out here again, honey. If it was left to me, this whole garden would have fallen apart."

Carol sets down the hose and joins her mother; together they sit in the rear of the yard, facing their own house. The hot sun bears down, making the water-beaded grass sparkle. Carol drains her soda down to the last clack of ice cubes. She and her mother sit in a relaxed silence.

And then: *Thoomp-Pop! Thoomp-thoomp-Pop!* The sound system starts up from the basement of Jamel Wilson's house across the way.

Carol groans. "Not again with the music! This is the third time this week."

Her mother snorts. "That's not music: it's garbage."

Carol snorts back. To her mother, any tunes after the heyday of Frank Sinatra and Rosemary Clooney are "garbage."

The beat pounds across the courtyard, overlaid with an angry voice chanting about "bitches" and "ho's."

"I'll tell you what that is," her mother says. "That's jungle music. That's all those coloreds know."

Carol thinks of Diana Ross, of Louis Armstrong and Stevie Wonder, but there's no point in trying to have a reasonable discussion. And—truth be told—even though she prides herself on having a broader view of life than her mother or many of the people she grew up with, this gangster rap tests her tolerance.

For no discernable reason the volume drops.

"I'll tell you another thing," her mother says, voice loud in the relative calm. "If this was the old neighborhood, by God we wouldn't have put up with this crap for five minutes! Some of the fellahs would've gone over there to have a conversation with that little hoodlum, and we'd never hear another peep out of that house."

Carol can't deny the truth of that. In the old neighborhood, where blacks were sometimes referred to as *mulignans*, for "eggplants," the "conversation" might have involved baseball bats.

"I don't understand it," her mother continues. "You look at the Koreans or the Chinese—they run their nice clean delis, and the kids grow up to be scientists or concert pianists. You take the Vietnamese and they own a business after just one generation over here. With all of these immigrants doing so well, why are these people such a mess?"

Carol sighs. "Ma, most of the blacks in America aren't immigrants. They didn't exactly volunteer to come here."

"Whose side are you on?" her mother snaps. She gnarls over in a coughing jag.

It never fails: just when Carol starts to like her again, the old lady trots out her nasty side. "I'm not going to argue with you," Carol says. She looks away and—through the tangle of vines and bushes in the rear of the garden—she sees Grace Howard standing in her own backyard.

"I'll tell you another thing," her mother starts up again. "If this was the old neighborhood"—

"Momma—just *shut up*."

CHAPTER TWENTY-ONE

EMPTY, THE AUDITORIUM FEELS CHILL AND MUSTY. GRACE SQUINTS to make sure her feet are safely placed as she descends toward the bright stage below.

Steve Bradley, head of the AV department, is bent over next to the podium, duct-taping a cable across the floor. As usual, his back pockets bulge with a collection of screwdrivers and connecting cables. He straightens to his full ungainly height of six-and-a-half feet.

"I'm just about there, Miz Howard. You wanna help me for a second? I'm gonna run up to the sound board—could you just say a few words into the mic so I can get my levels?"

"Everything else is ready?" she asks, not her usual calm self today. "Have you tested the video yet?"

"It's taken care of."

"Did you put—"

"The water and glasses are under the podium."

Grace opens her mouth, but Steve raises a hand to head her off. "No, there's no ice in it."

She nods. Everything will be just as Mr. Laidlaw likes it for his final speech to the employees of the Beardon Group.

"Big promotion day, huh?"

She shrugs modestly. "We'll see." Aside from the CEO's impending retirement, two other executives in the company have recently left their positions (one due to illness and one for a job offer in Washington). Despite Mr. Laidlaw's secrecy on the subject, everyone in the building expects him to announce the new promotions this afternoon.

"You gonna be the new head honcho, Miz Howard?"

She flushes. She wishes Charles were here to soothe her nerves and to share in her professional achievement—today she wouldn't even care about keeping their relationship a secret—but he has flown to Los Angeles on an unavoidable week-long business trip.

The AV man plops down off the stage and jogs up the auditorium steps.

"Oh," Grace calls out to his retreating back. "One more thing—"

"It's in the wings, stage left."

She smiles as she steps across the stage: such competence is a wonderful thing. Sure enough, a rolling cart waits in the wings with a swatch of satin draped over the top. Mr. Laidlaw's retirement gift. Grace lifts the fabric and peers underneath: a golden rococo swirl of waves and cherubs surrounds a stately clock, a keepsake originally given to George Washington by General Rochambeau of France. Price: forty-seven-thousand dollars (she knows because she signed off on the art consultant's purchase order).

* * *

Half an hour later the house lights are up as all of the New York employees of the Beardon Group troop in. The murmur of voices builds as the hall fills. Grace stands by the railing at the top, calling out greetings as old friends pass by. Here's Helen Chenosky from Mr. Gibson's office, limping slightly because of her bunions. And there's Meara Benko from Personnel, with whom she shared a tiny office back in the late seventies.

The lights go down and the voices subside. A screen slides down over the stage for a video tribute to the chief executive's career. "Thirty-five years ago Ed Laidlaw arrived at a small company with a modest tri-state portfolio of life insurance accounts," the narrator intones. "Today he leaves behind one of the world's leading insurance companies and a pioneer in many areas of finance and investment equity."

A series of photos flashes by: Mr. Laidlaw behind his desk, speaking before a crowd, shaking hands with several U.S. Presidents. Laughter rises from the audience as familiar faces appear in the background: a secretary here, a department head there. Standing in the back, Grace's heart warms with pride and—yes—a sense of belonging.

The lights come up and a line of young black boys files out on stage, marching stiffly in blue blazers, starched shirts, and striped ties. The South Bronx Boys Chorus, one of Mr. Laidlaw's pet charities. A young man steps out in front and lifts his hands, and they raise their sweet voices in song, first "Amazing Grace" and then "Many Rivers to Cross." Grace smiles down at the smallest boy as he squirms and digs a finger into the back of his collar.

Finally, Mr. Laidlaw crosses the stage to a burst of applause. He squares his shoulders, plants his hands in his pockets, and opens with a few jokes. He mentions his family, then wipes away a tear as he speaks gruffly of his love and attachment to this company, this group of wonderful people.

"I have one final responsibility here at the Beardon Group," he says. The audience goes still. "I would be remiss in my duties if I didn't make sure that I'm passing the torch along to someone who will assure the future of this company. Ladies and gentleman, I'd like to introduce the new CEO of the Beardon Group: Don Gibson."

The crowd applauds as Mr. Gibson makes his way up onto the stage, struggling to maintain a display of humility. The new chief raises a hand to quiet the room. "Thank you, Ed, thank you, everyone. I'll be talking to you all soon about my future plans for the Group, but first I'd like to take this opportunity to announce some other new appointments." He pulls a paper from his suit pocket.

As Grace expected, Mr. Conway will rise to the office vacated by Mr. Gibson. Mr. Perry will move behind Mr. Conway's desk. The list continues. Her heart races as she listens for her name.

Mr. Laidlaw proclaims that Director of Hospitality Alan DeBruyn will move up to a vice presidency in Public Relations. "And our new Director of Hospitality Services," he continues, "will be Cathy McManus."

Grace blinks in disbelief. The woman is reasonably competent, but she has been around for less than two years and has never arranged anything more complicated than an occasional luncheon.

Don Gibson takes a sip of water and continues. "Our new Assistant Director of Hospitality will be Grace Howard."

He announces several other promotions, but Grace is too stunned to take note.

And then the house lights go up and a hubbub of congratulations and speculation fills the room. The employees rise and mill in the aisles. A knot of well-wishers gathers around the new top executives. Across the room, Grace notices Cathy McManus, with her beaming young white face.

Meara Benko comes up the steps, but this time she ducks her head as she passes by. Other friends force pained smiles. Grace hurries through the swinging door, out into the lobby. She stabs at the elevator button; decides she can't bear to wait. She opens the fire door to the stairwell, climbs a flight of stairs, then stops short and sinks down onto the landing, the hollow tap of her heels against the stairs replaced by the pounding of her own blood in her ears.

Someone outside the company might think she should be happy. She's been lifted out of the secretarial world and onto an executive track; maybe she'll even get a raise. Yet anyone inside this hermetically sealed world can read between the lines. Grace Howard just got slapped down.

A bubble of grief rises in her chest. Thirty-five years she has been friends with Ed Laidlaw, or at least thought she was. Supported him, stayed late typing for him, even bought Christmas presents for Mrs. Laidlaw and the children. He knew she wanted the director's job, knew she deserved it. How could he do this to her?

She frowns at the wall. Maybe she was just imagining that she deserved the director's job. Maybe she's making a big deal out of a small thing. Maybe she *should* be happy about what she got.

She shakes her head: *No.* How many years has she stayed quiet, bitten her tongue, done the right thing? To make her father happy, even when he was thousands of miles away, even when he was gone? Her sister Amalie often got into trouble, but Grace was the good daughter, the steady reliable one, the one who never got angry, who patched things up and restored the family peace. The one who always worked the hardest. What has she sacrificed her life for in this guarded, responsible way?

* * *

Fifteen minutes later, after the auditorium—hopefully—will have cleared, she emerges from the stairwell and rides an empty elevator to her floor. She slips into her office, locks the door, and drops into her swivel chair.

She tries to call Charles in L.A., but a receptionist informs her that he has gone across town for a meeting.

She can't bear the cheery tropical fish swimming across her computer screen; she types in the command to turn off the machine and waits dully until it signals its approval: *It is now safe to shut down*.

* * *

The elevator door slides open at the forty-seventh floor and she moves quickly past the security desk, where the elderly white-haired guard gives her a friendly smile.

"How's it goin', Ms. Howard?"

"Not so good, Augie."

She strides along the Wedgewood-colored carpet, past the line of solemn portraits, through the French doors. This late in the day, Mr. Laidlaw's assistant will have gone home. There's no one to stop her as she pushes open the heavy mahogany door and enters the regal inner office, where Ed Laidlaw looks up from behind his desk, tie loosened, eyeglasses perched low on his nose.

"Grace," he says simply.

She reaches back for an armchair—she doesn't want to take her eyes off him—and sits. Now that she's come this far, she doesn't know what to say, where to begin. It doesn't matter: clearly the man knows what he has done. In the warm orange light of the antique desk lamp, he pushes his glasses up onto the bridge of his nose. Out through the corner windows of the dusky office, the sun is setting across the Hudson, bruising the sky with swathes of orange and purple and red.

"I wanted to tell you before," he says. "Listen—I've put in for a fifteen percent raise for you."

She sags back, feeling the cool satin arms of the chair. "You know I mentioned that I'd be interested in the director's job if it ever opened up. I've been wondering why you gave it to Cathy McManus instead. She's not a man. She hasn't been here longer; she just came two years ago. And she has less experience than I do. So where does that leave us? What's the only other difference between her and me?"

He leans forward across his elegant cherry-wood desk. "Don Gibson put together the new team. If it was up to me I would have made you a vice president, for chrissake." She watches him hold up his hands and lift his shoulders, a gesture so eloquent: *What can I do? I'm only a cog in a system that I didn't create* . . . He rises and walks to the window. "You know I've championed you here every step of the way—"

At this her voice finally rises. "Why would I need a champion, Edward?" She looks to his reflection in the glass. "I work twice as hard as anyone in this building. I'm the first one in, the last to leave. I have no children, hardly any life outside this place. And why?" She grips the arms of the chair. "I didn't want anyone to be able to say, 'Oh, she just got where she is through affirmative action, or because she's such a light-skinned woman, or—do you remember when you asked me to fire that young man from Corporate Dining last year, that young black manager? Do you know what he called me when he left? 'House nigger,' that's what. House nigger!"

"Grace, I—"

"Tell me something, Edward. Did Don Gibson say why he preferred Cathy McManus?"

He turns from the window with a pained look. "He said . . . he said that hospitality is essential to our business, and that some of our foreign clients might feel more comfortable—"

"*Foreign clients?* You're trying to blame this on foreigners?"

"I'm sorry, Grace. I know this may not seem very fair, but—" He stops abruptly. It occurs to her that maybe he has just envisioned a potential Equal Employment Opportunity Commission complaint.

She lowers her voice and leans forward, placing her hands on the edge of his desk. "Why don't you just say it, Edward? It's not so difficult. What's the real difference between her and me? Why don't you tell me? You're the one who's so good at spelling things out."

He lifts a paperweight off his desk, turns it over, and stares fixedly at the underside.

Grace hangs her head.

After then—because there doesn't seem to be anything more to say—they sit in a sad silence that, oddly, starts to feel almost companionable. After all, they've known each other for thirty-five years.

LaTisha gazes at her own moon face reflected in the window of the subway car.

"Sit down," her mother says and pushes her back against the scooped plastic seat. "Hold still." Mama's hands swoop down to solve the complex puzzle of her untied shoelaces. Over, under, looping—bow.

At the end of the car the connecting door clacks open, admitting the thunderous shuttling roar of the train, followed by a slight man stooped under the weight of a big cardboard box. The man smiles a friendly, squinting smile. The door clacks shut. Into the hollow puff of calm that follows, he shouts out in a high-pitched voice, tart as an unripe cherry.

"Two dollah! Two dollah!"

Rocking with the motion of the train, he leans back against the shiny pole in the center of the car. His arm disappears down into the depths of the box to dredge up a handful of beeping, blinking, whirring toys, which he scatters on the smudged linoleum floor. A little green alligator hunches its way across the aisle. A shiny robot flips backward. A tiny boy in a tiny black cap scoots forward carrying a tiny suitcase; he bumps against her mother's shoe.

LaTisha stares down, her little mouth an O, this world a giant hall of wonders.

CHAPTER TWENTY-TWO

TEE-ALI, WEARING HIS SHADES, ALMOST TRIPS AS HE COMES DOWN the dark basement steps, but Jamel is not about to laugh. Moving to the center of the room, he turns on a lamp over his amplifier and mixing board, spotlighting his sound system in all its glory. Tee-Ali and his friend Anthony don't say anything, but by the way they stick their hands in their pockets, Jamel can tell they're impressed. Tee-Ali is cocky enough on the street, but he seems cowed by this property, this house with a mother present. (His own mother kicked him out of their apartment for running with the drug crowd when he was thirteen.)

"Yo, son, don't be lookin' at the shit like that," Anthony says to Tee-Ali. "Jamel get robbed, he gonna send the police right over to your crib."

"Shut up, ponk." Tee-Ali scowls, but it's clear that his dark shades are hiding something weaker than his usual menace.

For a minute Jamel enjoys his old tormentor's jealous silence—after all, wasn't that one of the main reasons he bought this system?—but then he's surprised to find that he actually feels sorry for the kid.

"Yo, son," Anthony says—he calls everybody 'son'—"turn that bad boy on."

Jamel steps forward and picks up his all-time favorite CD, Wu-Tang Clan, *Enter the Wu-Tang (36 Chambers)*.

Tee-Ali, regaining a bit of his old confidence, snorts. "Why you playin' that? That shit is *old*."

Anthony chimes in. "Old? Yo, son, that shit is *Jurassic*."

They're right—the CD is from 1993—but Jamel pays no mind, just eases the disc into the player, turns up the bass. Then he settles down into his beanbag chair, as into a throne.

Anthony pulls a forty of Ballantine out of a paper bag and they pass it around.

The record starts with scratchy sampled dialogue from an old kung fu movie. Then, *bam*, the drums crash in, followed by the bold shouting voices of the Wu-Tang. Old horror-movie organ sounds weave in and out, horn and piano samples ride in over cymbal clash and echoing snare, over the beating muscle of the bass drum. This drum is the heartbeat, necessary as air—it gives time a rhythm, a shape, makes the world beat, move, swing. The track stops—time held still for one in-drawn breath—then the kung fu sample crops up again, followed by the sudden thunder of the drums. The music has layers upon layers, with odd little sounds hidden in the background, if you really pay attention.

Jamel closes his eyes. Welcome to the magic world of the Wu-Tang, of nines and swords, of Shaolin, of sexy seventies singers sampled. The soundtrack of life. Fuck the Fulton Street Mall—this turns the whole *planet* into Black People's World. These warriors are funny and angry and proud, heroes with guns who call life what it is, who never, ever Yassuh to the police, to the Ricky managers, the Mr. Ks. They're heroes, black heroes for once, geniuses with the sampler and the spoken word.

Jamel sits back in his chair, sipping beer and basking in the admiration of his visitors.

After a few minutes the overhead light snaps on. He pushes himself up out of the chair and lowers the volume. "Yo!" he shouts toward the top of the stairs. "Why you do that?"

"*Jamel*," his mother calls. "You best get up here. And turn that music off."

"Wait up," Jamel says, turning to Tee-Ali and Anthony. "I be right back." He turns the amplifier off and trudges upstairs, annoyed.

His mother stands in the hallway, blocking the open front door with her body, but Jamel can see two cops standing outside under the bright stoop light. He groans in frustration. What is *wrong* with his neighbors? He can't understand it. Not only do they hate music, but it's as if they've made a concerted campaign to ruin his life. What has he done to deserve this?

One of the cops, a stocky black man with a slightly Asian-looking face, takes off his cap and tucks it under his arm as Jamel steps outside past his mother. The other Five-O is a woman, a pretty young Latino whose black hair gleams in the light.

The man does the talking. "You live here, son?"

Jamel clears his throat uneasily. "Is there a problem?"

"We've gotten a couple of calls from your neighbors about excessive noise. You have a stereo downstairs?"

"Aw, *man.*" Jamel shakes his head in disgust. "It ain't even nine o'clock. Don't I got a legal right to play music inside my own house?"

"Yes, you do, but not to bother the neighbors."

His mother steps forward, arms crossed. "These people"—she tilts her head toward the new neighbors' house—"they're very uptight. Always complainin' about somethin'. He wasn't even playin' it loud."

The policeman exchanges a wry look with his partner. "Well, ma'am, you didn't hear us until we rang five times."

"I don't hear too good," says Melba, face tightening for battle. "Now why you bothering us?"

Jamel decides he better step in and smooth things over. "All right, officer," he says. "No problem. I'll turn it down. Okay?"

The cop scratches the back of his neck, surprised by this sudden favorable turn in the negotiation. "We'd appreciate it," he says. "Thank you for your time." He and his partner nod goodnight, and then they go down the stoop and out the gate.

Jamel and his mother watch as the squad car disappears.

"We got a right," Jamel mutters.

His mother nods. "You best believe it, baby."

* * *

Jamel rejoins his guests down in the basement.

"Yo, son," says Anthony. "What up?"

"Nuh'in," Jamel answers. He pulls the master volume of his system down just a hair, then hits Play.

CHAPTER TWENTY-THREE

THE GRASS IS BROWNING. THROUGH THE CHAIN-LINK FENCE, CAROL watches the Paladinos' lawn baking, crisping in the heat. Upstate, the reservoirs are dangerously low, and the Governor has mandated conservation measures—no watering of lawns—but Carol can't stop herself from wetting down her garden. She hears her plants crying out—how can she not respond?

As she crouches down to pull a few crackly weeds away from the base of her begonias, she can feel the sweat beading on her lower back, soaking into the waistband of her shorts. For the past three nights she and her mother have been sleeping on mattresses dragged onto the linoleum floor of the kitchen, where it's cooler than upstairs.

Next door, Charlie Paladino comes out to trim his lawn with an old push mower. He's old and stocky, his hair white and unruly; there's something boyish about the way a cowlick sticks up behind.

"How ya doin'?" he says, noticing Carol.

"Not too bad," she answers, discovering to her surprise that she actually means it. Recently she has felt as if she has been waking up. Just yesterday she replaced the tattered sponge next to the kitchen sink, threw out some old bras and bought new ones, scrubbed the mildew off the shower curtain in the bathroom. She thinks about her hurt, festering all winter, brewing poisons. A well-planned garden must tilt away from the house, so that the drainage will not seep in.

She has found herself able to think of her husband more objectively, to recognize his weaknesses. All that time they were together, she had been thinking of him as a war victim, but she realizes that those troubles didn't necessarily make him a better person. He became the man he was before Bosnia was ripped apart. She keeps coming back to a comment he made as they danced at her cousin's wedding: "The war," he had said, "was not all of life." She feels confident now that, if she can just see him one last time, she'll be able to put the whole matter to rest.

Diagonally across the court a door opens and one of the new neighbors comes out. Kristin, the wife. Seeing Carol, she offers a perfunctory smile and then bends down to examine her sad little portulacas, their leaves drooping in the heat. Carol notes with some amusement that she's wearing special gardening pants, probably from some fancy catalog. They keep to themselves, this couple. They have their own friends, women in smart outfits who visit with their babies in the afternoons, or couples who come on the weekend to barbecue and drink imported beer.

* * *

Mitchell comes out of the dry cleaners holding his plastic-tented work shirts close to his body. He trots across Court Street because he doesn't want to be seen: there's another shop at the other end of the block run by a Korean family who are much friendlier than the proprietors of the store he's just left, but this more modern operation can do the shirts overnight.

He ducks down a side street. Two blocks away the dull red towers of the Wysocki Houses rise into the afternoon light. In nine months of living in the neighborhood, he has never actually walked by the projects, but he comes close enough this Sunday afternoon to hear loudspeakers booming out over the rooftops, some sort of rally echoing from the projects' inner courtyards. The words are indistinguishable, yet the tone comes through: proud, offended, angry. Is it a religious gathering? A political event? He's not going close enough to find out, but ever since his night at the police station he has become oddly aware of this other world. It's one thing to read editorials in the *Times* about the racial and economic divide in the country—it's another to think that there's a place just one block away from his house that is forbidden to him, a mysterious alternate nation. If there were some way to become invisible, he'd like to go into the projects and see for himself what life inside is like.

As he veers away from the projects and walks down his own street, the unmistakable thud of his neighbor's sound system booms out of the open cellar door. He groans as he pushes open his front gate. Inside his house, he's greeted by the revivifying cool of the air-conditioning, but even the closed windows can't block out the sound, this music stripped of all melody or harmony, boiled down to a dull subterranean pounding through the floor and walls.

He presses a palm against one eye in frustration. "Goddamn punk." It's a failure of imagination, an inability on the kid's part to imagine himself in anyone else's place, or even to sense that his actions have an impact beyond his own little world.

Mitchell is about to walk into the kitchen, but stops short at the sight of a stranger sitting with Kristin at the table, a big, rather horsey-looking woman with teased-up black hair.

"Honey, this is Carol, from across the way," Kristin says, and now he recognizes their neighbor from the other side of the courtyard.

"I'm Mitchell," he says, draping his dry cleaning over the back of a chair and reaching out to shake hands.

"Pleased to meetcha," Carol replies, feeling clumsy as she reaches across the table and accepts his uncertain grip. His hair lies limp across his forehead and there's some pale stubble on his chin; it's the weekend. Milosz was more handsome. This Mitchell wears sweatpants without shorts over them—she looks away. The kitchen seems so bright: it's not just the fresh white paint, but the cheery hanging planters in the windows, the airy blue-and-white-striped curtains in the window, folded and draped like in a magazine. She's glad that they're sitting here to talk, rather than in her mother's kitchen with its stained wallpaper, shabby dishtowels, uneven floor.

"Can I get you some more iced tea?" Kristin asks, leaning across the table with a pitcher filled with real tea and thin-sliced lemon wedges (no "flavor-crystals" here!). She turns to her husband. "We've been talking about the noise."

Mitchell sighs as he sits down. "I went over there the other day— very politely—to ask the kid to turn it down, and his mother told me that this isn't Connecticut. She walked away from me."

"That would be Melba," Carol says.

"You know her?"

"We used to talk sometimes, over the fences."

Mitchell brightens. "Do you think you could speak to her about this noise business? We'd sure appreciate it."

Carol sets her empty glass down and winces. "I don't think I'd have any better luck than you did."

"Why not? I mean, if you know her and all . . ."

"A couple years back we had a fight. She had some grape vines that were coming over into my yard, and one day I decided to trim them, just on my side, of course, and she came out and started shouting at me. It ended up, she called me a 'white bitch.' Ever since then, we don't talk."

Through the kitchen wall, the music fades out. All present hold their breath. A second later—*boom Pop!, boom boom Pop!*—it starts up again. The window buzzes.

Mitchell shakes his head. "We have to do something about this. We can't use the garden, I can't concentrate on my work—"

"He called the police," Kristin says.

Carol raises her eyebrows. "Really? What happened?"

"They didn't show up," Mitchell replies glumly.

"It was a Friday night," Kristin adds.

Carol sets down her glass. "This reminds me of a situation we had here six or seven years ago."

Mitchell leans forward expectantly. There's something invigorating about having contact with this woman, a real Brooklynite, and he's excited to be let in on the secrets of the block, this world that existed long before he and his wife arrived.

"You know the Chapins' house?" Carol says. Seeing the couple's blank look, she adds, "Three doors down from you, the gray house with the wooden deck?"

Husband and wife nod.

"Well, before the Chapins moved in, there was this couple living there, middle-aged, respectable-looking people—the husband worked for the Transit Authority. But at night, after his wife went to sleep, the guy would turn on the lights in the living room and pull open the curtains—you know how they have those whaddayacall'em, French doors? He'd walk out in his bathrobe, and you'd see him looking out the back, and then he'd, well, he'd expose himself."

"Expose himself?" Kristin says.

"Yeah, you know—show his *thing*. This would happen a couple times a month."

"What did you do?" asks Mitchell, wide-eyed.

"Well, a couple of the neighbors on this side of the yard got together to talk about it. We didn't really want to call the cops, 'cause it would probably ruin the guy's marriage and maybe he'd lose his job, and it wasn't exactly *hurting* anybody—there were no young kids over here back then. But we were getting pretty tired of seeing this guy's privates every time we looked out the back."

"What happened?"

"Well, we thought of this, and we thought of that. One of the guys at my office said he'd dress up as a cop and come over and stand in my window and point at the guy and maybe that would scare him off. He never got the costume together, though. My mother said this would never have happened in the old neighborhood."

"Why not?" Kristin asks.

Carol rotates her neck uncomfortably. "We used to live in Carroll Gardens. There were some powerful, uh, *families* there, if you know what I mean. My mother said they would've come over and tied the guy's prick in a knot. If you'll excuse the expression."

"So did he keep doing it?"

"For a while, yeah. But then finally my neighbor next door, he's a camera buff, he took a picture of the guy with one of those zoom lenses and he dropped it through the mail slot with a note saying that the next picture would be addressed to the wife. A few months later, those people moved out, and the Chapins moved in."

Mitchell takes a moment to consider the story, trying to figure how it might apply to the current situation. There doesn't seem to be any way to shame or blackmail the kid out of playing the stereo—after all, his own mother seems to approve of the obnoxious behavior. "Those *families* in Carroll Gardens—what would it take to get one of them to help out with this situation?" He follows the question with a weak laugh to demonstrate that he's kidding. Half-kidding. (If the police won't help out, they may be left with very few options.) He slips into a fantasy scenario: an unmarked envelope filled with cash, a quick kneecap job, absolute peace and quiet for the rest of their stay in the neighborhood . . .

"You wouldn't want to mess with that," Carol replies, bringing him back to earth. "Once they do a favor, you never know what kind of favor they're going to want back."

"Of course," Mitchell says, quickly.

"Maybe we should start a phone chain," says Kristin.

She says it with a cool authority that impresses Carol; it would take a lot to make this woman break a sweat. "What do you mean?"

"Well, if only one neighbor calls the police, they can probably ignore it, but if a lot of us get together every time the noise starts, and we all call . . ."

"That might work," Carol says. She isn't too thrilled about making such a fuss, calling in the cops and all, but then she'd like some peace and quiet in the garden, too. She pauses to consider who else might be interested in this group action. The Chapins, certainly: they've already complained to her about the noise. The Zellers, three doors down . . . She thinks of Grace across the way: what would she say? And would asking put her in a difficult position, her being black and all?

CHAPTER TWENTY-FOUR

"MIZZES HOWARD?"

Grace looks up to see a shy Latina waiter from Corporate Dining, standing outside her office door.

"Yes?"

"The chef, he send you son'thing." The woman wheels in a cart topped with a beautifully laid-out lunch and a small bouquet of flowers in a vase.

Grace rises and picks up a little card next to the entree plate. "It should have been you," it says.

"Mizzes Howard? Are you all righ'?"

Grace nods, too moved to answer. All week, gifts have been making their way to her office: cards, flowers, a colorful scarf, little tokens from her colleagues at the Beardon Group, expressing their solidarity and sharing her dismay over her non-promotion. Even Helen Chenosky, now secretary to the new CEO, put herself on the line by coming by to commiserate. (Mr. Laidlaw, thankfully, has taken the week off, so Grace hasn't had to deal with seeing him around the office.) A couple of the younger secretaries have been whispering that she should put in a complaint to the Equal Employment Opportunity Commission. In her angriest moments, Grace can derive some satisfaction from picturing Mr. Gibson and Ed Laidlaw being served with subpoenas, but she feels that the ultimate loser of a lawsuit—even if she won it—would be herself. It has taken her over three decades to make herself a home in this company and such an action would cut her off irrevocably.

But then, perhaps this home has already been ruined for her. Many times each day she finds herself wondering, *Did I imagine this? Am I being too sensitive? Could it be that I'm not right for the job?* She thinks of her father and feels ashamed, as if she let him down. And she is unwilling to bring any unfavorable publicity to the Beardon Group; she worries that harming the company might bring grief to her coworkers.

She wheels the cart over to her desk, impressed by the chef's elegant presentation. On the windowsill stands a big bouquet of roses, courtesy of Charles Matthews, still in Los Angeles. He offered to fly back right away, to talk to Mr. Gibson himself, but she told him that she didn't want him to jeopardize his position on the board.

She picks halfheartedly at the food, then sets down her fork and stares out the window. It looks like another scorching day outside and she worries about her garden.

* * *

Friday night she's still in a state of shock. Saturday, she stays inside her air-conditioned house, out of the heat, numb.

Sunday morning she remains in bed, mourning her ruined hopes and thinking, thinking: remembering Candace Walker standing in the cafeteria, turning to her in guilty shock; remembering Edward Laidlaw in his office that terrible afternoon; he had barely even pretended to deny his betrayal. She thinks of her father, of his unswerving dedication to doing right, thinks of him with love, yet wonders if his clear-cut sense of morality has not left her in some way unprepared for the muddy world. The compassion of her co-workers goes some way toward preventing her from giving up on people in general, but all in all she would like to just stay in bed and avoid human contact.

The doorbell rings. Wary, she pulls on her robe and trudges downstairs. Through the frosted glass inset in the door, she recognizes the big frame of Carol Fasone. She opens the door, noting that her neighbor seems less pale, less hangdog than she has all spring—she looks like a drooping plant finally given water.

"Hi," Carol says. "I hope I'm not bothering you."

"Not at all," Grace replies, polite as ever.

Her neighbor looks uneasily down the street. "Could I come in for a minute?"

"Of course. I'm sorry," Grace replies. She leads Carol into her kitchen and gestures to a chair. "Can I get you something to drink?"

"No—I just stopped by." Carol sits but fidgets, picking up a salt-shaker and then setting it down. "It's incredible how much your roses are blooming this year."

"Yes. I'm very pleased."

"Mine aren't doing so well. I think the heat is getting to them."

Grace sits patiently, waiting to discover the real reason for the visit.

"Well," Carol says. "There's actually something else I wanted to talk to you about."

"Yes?" Grace says, lifted by curiosity out of her own circling thoughts.

"It's about the noise situation. You know . . ."

"Noise?" Grace asks. She realizes now why her neighbor is here and why Carol seems so uncomfortable, but she feels disinclined to make this easier for her.

"The music. I'm sure you must have noticed. From the Wilson's house?"

"Yes?"

"Well," Carol says, scratching the back of her hand, "I had a talk with some of the neighbors. I mean, they came to me about it. You see, they've talked to Jamel several times, and they even went to ask his mother if she'd tell him to turn it down, but she, well—she tried to make it seem like a racial thing."

"Racial?"

"Yeah, like maybe she figures this is about white people not liking rap music, or something. But it's not. I mean, it's just about being good neighbors, right?"

Grace sits, impassive. She remembers Carol sobbing in her arms in the Botanic Garden, remembers her whole heartbreaking story—but she also remembers Carol's mother in the backyard, going on about "those people" and about how "the old neighborhood" would have dealt with the noise.

"So anyhow," Carol continues hurriedly, "they want to organize the block to do something about it."

"Organize?"

"Yeah, like get a phone chain to call the police if this keeps up. Or maybe go down to the precinct and talk to the Community Patrol officers about it."

"You want me to participate?"

"If you want to. I mean, I'm sure the noise must bother you when you're in your garden. And, to tell the truth, it would be great if we could show that this isn't a racial thing. That *all* the neighbors are bothered by this."

Grace looks down at her hands. She opens them and considers the lines in her palms. She imagines her blood circulating, pictures tiny bubbles starting to rise from the bottom of a pan. "I think," she says in a tight, closed voice she barely recognizes as her own, "that I would rather not."

"Not *what*?"

"Participate."

Carol stops fidgeting and stares in surprise.

"But why? It must bother you, too."

"I choose not to," Grace says, in lieu of all the reasons percolating up inside.

Carol scratches the side of her head, looks down at the floor. She waits for a minute, then pushes awkwardly away from the table and rises. "Well. I'm sorry you feel this way. Of course, if you change your mind . . ."

"I don't think so."

Carol stands there, fingering the collar of her sweatshirt. She looks hurt. "I suppose I better go."

Grace doesn't respond. After the front door closes, she stands behind it, gripping the cool glass of the knob. The muscles in her arm tense and she almost shakes with all the things she didn't allow herself to express.

"Not a racial thing," her neighbor had said. It's funny, she thinks, but in all the years they've known each other, they have never had a frank discussion about race. Once, she remembers, Carol made a big deal about how much she enjoyed a concert of the Alvin Ailey Dance Company that her office had sponsored—made too big a deal.

Grace drifts into the kitchen and washes some dishes, her thoughts churning like the hot soapy water. She pauses, a dishtowel in one hand and a glass in the other, and looks out the window at the courtyard withering in the summer heat. She looks at Carol's house across the way.

You listen to your mother go on about "jungle music" and "the niggers" all day—and I should believe you haven't been affected? Scratch deep enough and the poison is always there.

She looks up at the massive brick buildings of the Wysocki Houses rising over the back of the courtyard and begins to compose a mental memo, copies to Carol Fasone, to the Bretts, the Marshalls, the Zellers.

You-all want to organize. To get together. Make phone calls. Expend great energy. All because one silly child wants to play some music. Is this what you choose to get upset about, when just around the corner there is a giant housing project sinking under the weight of poverty and crime and your neglect? Where families are going hungry every night? Where children are killing each other in their despair? Where are the phone calls? Who is organizing about that?

She dries the last dish and leaves the kitchen, climbs the stairs to her bedroom. She should go out—there are so many personal errands to run on the weekends—but she's weary, too weary, consumed by the bitter letter growing in her head. Copies to Candace Walker, to Edward Laidlaw . . .

What are they all complaining about? you ask. Black people have just as much chance now as anybody else. They can go as far as their willingness to study and work can take them. Look at the Cosbys. Look at Michael Jordan, Johnnie Cochran, Oprah. Doctors. Lawyers. Happy families. What are they so angry about?

Yes, you say, slavery was a terrible thing, but we had nothing to do with making these streets, these projects; this all happened long ago.

It's time to put the past behind us and recognize our common human-
ity. Aren't we all the same, really, under the skin? These people just
need to find their own pride and initiative.

Well, didn't I work hard? Didn't I burn my stomach up with worry
and uncertainty and the anger I never let spill? Wasn't I quiet and
reasonable and not-like-most-of-your-kind enough?

She sits on the edge of the bed, on a quiet-patterned floral bedspread, gazing out the window at the broiling sky.

One black boy plays his stereo and you're ready to organize. Ready
to take action. Well, I won't join your phone chain. Won't go to the
police with you. Won't smooth the waters, be the token reasonable
black.

Let that music rattle your lawns and keep you up at night until you
think about what's wrong with this picture. Let that boy go out in his
yard and shake his little black behind. Let him dance.

CHAPTER TWENTY-FIVE

A WARM SMELL OF BREAKFAST RISES IN THE KITCHEN. MITCHELL folds an omelette, pleased with the perfect light browning of the top, and slides it onto a plate. An omelette isn't exactly haute cuisine, but he can picture himself standing happily in front of a restaurant stove.

"Honey, it's ready," he calls to his wife, then sits at the kitchen table and props the sports section open against a cereal box.

Thoomp Pop! Thoomp thoomp Pop!

"Shit!" He stands and looks out the kitchen window. No one is in his neighbor's yard but the music still punches out into the court. Mitchell trots through his apartment to the front window and peers out. Two doors down, the kid is standing in front of his stoop, blithely hosing down the walk while the noise thunders out of the open cellar door. The boy is wearing only sweatpants; he idly scratches his bare stomach and adjusts the sprayer.

"Not a care in the world," murmurs Mitchell. "You little *fucker.*" He's gripped by an urge to charge out of his house and go over there and strangle the kid. Although they're about the same height, the teenager's pretty skinny, and Mitchell has righteous anger on his side. But who might be hanging out in the basement? He wouldn't want to tangle with the kid's mother. And he remembers some of the tough-looking kids he's seen hanging around—who knows what kind of thugs this Jamel is tangled up with?

He shuts the windows and turns on the air-conditioning, but the music still throbs through the walls. He paces to and fro, pausing now and then to look out the window and see if the kid is still there. He clenches his fists so hard that his nails dig into his palms. It would be bad enough to be exposed to such noise out on the streets, but this is his home—his personal space—that's being messed with here. Worst of all, it's an invasion not only of his house but the inside of his head. He has tried earplugs, but they don't work; it's not a question of hearing, really, but of a deeper vibration that thuds into his entire body. It's like a lab experiment to see what will happen to a rat if it has no control over its environment. Once that pounding starts, it's impossible to think about anything else. Things have escalated to the point that his weekends and evenings are ruined even when the music *isn't* playing: in the valleys of quiet, he's obsessed with wondering when it's going to start up again. The anger builds and builds with no hope of release, a circle being drawn tighter and tighter until he feels like his very veins will explode.

Visions of revenge consume him. A Mafia contract seems like the neatest solution, but it's obviously only a fantasy. Still, maybe he could hire some big guys to just go in and smash the kid's sound system. Or how about hiring some kind of DJ with a giant sound system to set up speakers right here? Give the little punk a taste of his own medicine. Blast him with some Wagner, maybe—"The Ride of the Valkyries" that they played from the helicopters in *Apocalypse Now*, or some Lynyrd Skynrd. No, best of all—make the kid listen to a Beach Boys record, day in, day out.

"Your omelette's getting cold," Kristin calls from the kitchen.

Mitchell stomps back in. "The little asshole's at it again."

"Just try to ignore it," Kristin says. "You're letting him get to you."

"I can't ignore it. I can't think when that noise is blasting. I can't even concentrate on the damned sports section. *He* doesn't have to worry about thinking. Little jungle bunny probably can't even read."

"Mitchell!"

"What?"

"I don't like that kind of talk."

"Well I don't like to put up with this Chinese water torture." Mitchell realizes that his new ideological sensitivities seem to be going down the tubes, but he feels justified.

Kristin frowns.

"What?" he says. "I'm supposed to believe that he has to behave this way because he's 'disadvantaged'? Because of *slavery*, or something? I didn't have anything to do with slavery! Anyway, this isn't a poor, downtrodden ghetto kid we're talking about here. They have a *car*. His house is the same as ours, for chrissakes! And his stereo is obviously ten times the size of mine. Why should I feel sorry for him?"

"Let's just eat," she says, setting a quart of orange juice on the table.

"Why does that kid's mother let him just hang out all day? He should be in school, or working. At his age, I was working my butt off."

"You had a job?"

"Well, not a job exactly, but I was prepping for my SATs, and that certainly was work."

He thinks he sees a faint smirk pass across his wife's face. "How do you suppose they can afford a house like that?" he says, changing tack. "I bet his mother's some kind of welfare cheat." He can recognize in this comment the echo of his own father's smug voice, but he presses on.

"She's not on welfare," Kristin replies coolly. "She works for a real estate agency."

"How do you know that?"

"Carol told me yesterday."

"You mean that woman who lives across the court?"

"She came over for a cup of coffee."

"She did?"

"Why do you sound so surprised? I need some distraction around here."

Distraction? Mitchell thinks. They should go up to the bedroom right now for a little distraction. Make a baby. That's what they should be concentrating on. Buying tiny outfits and picking out names. Not stressing out over this ridiculous bullshit, some idiot teenager holding the whole block hostage.

He picks up the phone.

"What are you doing?"

"I'm using your idea. Let's phone the neighbors and get everybody to call the cops."

* * *

Five minutes later he has managed to reach Carol Fasone and two other neighbors. Then he calls the precinct and delivers his complaint. And half an hour later—by which time his omelette has grown rubbery from neglect, since he can't bear to leave the front window—a police cruiser actually pulls up in front of the kid's house.

"Yesss!" Mitchell hisses. He watches with glee as two jaded-looking cops climb out of the car and make their stiff-legged way up to the front of the kid's house; he jumps with joy when they push open the front gate. Though he stands on tiptoe and cranes his neck, he loses sight of them after they mount the first couple steps of the stoop. A minute later, the bass ceases thudding through the wall. The cops reappear, amble back to their car, and drive off.

Mitchell returns to the kitchen and reports to his wife. "This is beautiful!" he says, grinning. He sits and prods his share of the omelette with a fork. "I'll make another one—you want more?"

He stands and is scraping the cold omelette into the garbage when—*Thoomp Pop! Thooomp-thoomp Pop!*—the music starts up with even greater force. The blood drains from his face. He turns and smashes his fist into the wall.

"Mitchell!"

He grabs his pained hand and considers the dent he's made in the wallboard.

"What's *wrong* with you?" Kristin says.

He answers through clenched teeth. "Well, aside from the fact that I may have broken my hand, I've got a really nice headache from that little fucker's noise."

"You're starting to scare me. It's not *that* bad."

"Why can't you take my side?" he answers. "Just once?"

* * *

Ellen Chapin pulls into a Visitors' parking space just down the street from the precinct house. She gets out and holds the door open while Mitchell tumbles out, cramped from being pressed into the backseat of her little rusty Subaru with Kristin and Carol Fasone, who takes up a considerable amount of space. As he stands on the sidewalk rolling his shoulders to get the kinks out, Ellen locks up. She's a lean and prematurely gray mother of two. On the ride over, he was not surprised to learn that she attended Woodstock—the woman operates a pottery studio and still wears tie-dyed clothing.

Mrs. Zeller climbs out of the passenger seat. Her first name is Marnie, or Chernie, or something—he didn't quite catch it during the round of introductions and now he's embarrassed to ask. She looks to be in her mid-sixties, dressed in clothes that look too warm for the weather.

He feels a bit self-conscious, the only man in the group. (Mr. Zeller and Ellen's boyfriend or whatever he is, begged off for various reasons.) Anyhow, as Ellen pointed out, the women have the biggest stake in this visit, since they're at home most of the time, subjected to the music during the day as well as on weekends.

On the ride over, Mitchell reflected on an irony of the situation: before this problem came up, he'd rarely had the occasion to say more than five words to any of these neighbors.

Together the group shuffles into the police station. As Kristin approaches the front desk to inform the duty officer that they've come for their meeting with the Community Patrol sergeant, Mitchell scans the lobby, wondering if Detective Schimek might pass by. But Schimek is nowhere to be seen, nor the pretty Latina officer with the red lips who directed him upstairs during his last visit here.

A squat bald cop with one arm in a cast leads the group down a hall to a back office. Mitchell holds the door for his wife and the other women, then follows them inside.

"I'll be right with you," says a black cop seated behind an old Buick of a desk. The plastic sign on top reads "Sergeant Emerson." The officer has a telephone receiver clamped between his chin and shoulder while he jots something on the outside of a folder. He looks about forty, a roly-poly guy with the resonant voice and jovial manner of a TV weatherman. Wow, Mitchell thinks. "Emerson"—he hadn't figured the guy would be black. How are they going to explain the racial side of the problem now?

Sergeant Emerson waves the group into a semicircle of chairs around the desk. "Send Griffin and Garvey over to get a report," he says into his phone. "I'll come by tomorrow to make sure everything's calmed down." He hangs up and stands to greet the group.

"Thank you all for coming by. I understand you've been having some problems over in"—he looks at a note on his desk—"Boerum Hill."

There's a pause—they hadn't discussed who would act as spokesperson.

Carol shifts her purse in her lap; she has no intention of singling herself out by being the first to speak. She's not happy with the nuisance, but these neighbors act as if the music was a personal affront. Despite their initial awkwardness, they sit with an aura of rectitude and entitlement: *We are upper-middle-class people and we demand our taxes' worth.*

It's Kristin who responds. "That's right," she tells the officer. "There's a youth on the block who plays his stereo at a deafening level. Of course we might tolerate the occasional party, but he likes to disturb the block at all times of the day or night."

Carol winces inside at her neighbor's speech. *Might tolerate.* Kristin sounds so prissy that Carol wonders if she might cause the sergeant to dismiss their complaint as class-bound arrogance. She wishes Grace Howard was here. Ever since she asked her neighbor to get involved, they haven't exchanged more than a token hello over the back fences. It hardly seems possible, but could Grace have been so offended by her request that it will affect their friendship permanently? It occurs to her that perhaps her neighbor refused to cooperate because she was upset by Carol's mother's comments in the backyard. Maybe, she muses, she should have apologized for what her mother said—should have brought the subject out into the open.

"Have you spoken to the young man about the matter?" the sergeant asks.

"Oh, yes," says Mitchell. "We tried to be calm and reasonable about it, but they—his mother—wanted to . . ." His face contorts as he struggles with his words. "She tried to turn it into a racial issue."

"The family's Afro-American?"

Mitchell nods.

It seems to Carol that the neighbors are holding their breath, waiting to see how the officer will respond.

Sergeant Emerson takes in the information without any noticeable discomfort. He leans back in his chair. "Well, this is unfortunate, but we see this situation all the time. You shouldn't try to confront the family directly; that's our job. I have to tell you frankly that it's very difficult to deal with a noise problem. We'd have to catch the perpetrator in the act, but unfortunately the police department is not equipped with noise meters. One thing you can do is call the Department of Environmental Control and see if you can get someone to come over and take a reading."

"Does this mean that you can't help us?" says Mrs. Zeller.

"No, ma'am," replies the sergeant. "We'll do everything we can. First of all, I'll instruct the Community Patrol officer for your neighborhood to swing by as often as he can to listen for the noise."

"But you're *the police*," Mitchell says. "Can't you just order him to turn it down?"

"I'm afraid it's not that simple. There's a civil ordinance on the books regarding noise, but it's difficult for us to enforce. One problem is that the perpetrators will often turn the music down when they see us coming."

"Perhaps you don't realize how serious this problem is," Mrs. Zeller says. "We can't even go out in our gardens anymore."

"Believe me," Sergeant Emerson says, "I sympathize with you. I had a similar problem in my own neighborhood with a Russian family who were always blasting the Bee Gees in their backyard."

"What did you do?" Mitchell asks.

"We got lucky," Emerson replies. "They were having problems meeting the rent and they moved out."

* * *

Ellen Chapin parks her car a couple of streets away from their block. They agree that it's probably best not to be seen as a group: if Jamel and his friends witness them banding together, who knows what reprisals they might be capable of? That thought has evidently occurred to others not present today. Mitchell had called the Paladinos about the meeting, but they refused to attend, saying that they didn't want to get involved. He wanted to point out that they were "involved" whether they liked it or not, but he didn't get a chance to argue. He imagined the family hiding behind their lace curtains like scared townspeople in some old Western.

"Well," he says now, "that sergeant seemed like a decent guy. I think we might have made some progress. Maybe having a black officer on our side will help to defuse the racial part of this business."

"We can only hope," says Mrs. Zeller.

The group of neighbors breaks up and goes their separate ways.

As Mitchell and his wife round the corner and head down their block, a muted thumping sounds in the distance. As he approaches the usual source of the noise, he sees Jamel out front hosing down the sidewalk. He scowls at the boy, but Kristin grabs his arm and pulls him inside their house.

* * *

"This is Schimek," says the gruff voice on the other end of the line.

Mitchell clears his throat. "I don't know if you'll remember me— my name is Mitchell Brett and I was mugged last fall over in Boerum Hill—"

"Mr. Brett, yeah, sure I remember. What can I do for you?"

Mitchell explains the situation with the noise.

"Have you talked to the Community Patrol officers?"

"I just came from there. They said they'd try to help, but they sounded kind of vague. I was wondering if you might have some advice."

Schimek snorts. "If this was my neighborhood, we'd have taken care of the problem right away."

"How?" Mitchell says eagerly.

"I'm sorry, Mr. Brett, I'm afraid I can't really say. You should go ahead and work with your local CPOP officers. Good luck to ya. I'm sorry, but I have to go out on a call now."

Mitchell hangs up the phone bitterly. He walks through his house and looks out the front window at Jamel Wilson, calmly hosing down the sidewalk while the music slams away behind him.

I hope you die, Mitchell mutters. I hope you get in a fight with one of your drug-dealer buddies and he shoots you. And I'll walk by your house and I won't give a good goddamn, because you people don't give a damn about anybody else.

CHAPTER TWENTY-SIX

AS SOON AS THEY GET ON THE SUBWAY, LATISHA BEGINS TO SQUIRM and fret in her mother's lap. Shanice bends down, her marcelled hair gleaming in the fluorescent light; under the racketing of the train, Jamel can just make out the rhyme she recites to try to calm her daughter:

Had a little chickie
Wouldn't lay a egg
Poured hot water
All up and down his leg
Little chickie cry
Little chickie beg
Little chickie lay me a hard-boil egg

Tisha, unpacified, wriggles to be let down. Her little face puckers into a whimper.

Jamel watches from his perch across the aisle. For some reason, Shanice has warmed to him in the last several weeks, easing up on her usual practice of jabbing him with her sharp wit every time she comes over with the baby. And today, on her birthday, since he has consented to her request for a family-style outing, she's been out-and-out friendly. Which is why this may be a good day to make a special proposition.

Tisha twists around in her mother's arms, whining and so miserable-looking that Jamel starts to feel her discomfort as if it were his own. He opens a bag of barbecued potato chips and picks a small one, then leans across the aisle to offer it to his daughter. Tisha grasps the chip carefully in her tiny hand, lifts it to her mouth, gums contentedly. Every time she smiles at Jamel it makes him feel like he's been given a gift.

He consults the subway map. He rarely comes into Manhattan. The complicated trains, strange crowds, his lack of knowledge about which neighborhoods are friendly or not—even when he's on his own, the city makes him uneasy, but today he's especially anxious.

* * *

In the elevator, packed in with a group of tourists murmuring to each other in all sorts of odd languages, he holds Tisha while Shanice searches through her shoulder bag for a bottle.

"During our journey to the Observatory of the Empire State Building we will rise eighty-six floors," intones the elevator operator, obviously bored out of his mind. "Although this elevator will take you one thousand and fifty feet above Manhattan, it can make the trip in less than a minute."

"Trip down only take five seconds," says Jamel, feeling enough confidence to try to impress his fellow riders.

"*Shush*," says Shanice.

Jamel looks around: out of maybe thirty people, only two others are black, and they're speaking in a foreign language. Maybe they're Africans.

"For twelve dollars each, we could've seen a movie," he tells Shanice as they disembark. "This shit best be worth it, or I'm gonna aks for my money back."

As they step out onto the observation deck, though, his cockiness turns into awe. Beneath the huge open bowl of the sky, the earth actually curves along the horizon. He has only been this high up once, when he was a little kid and his family flew down South to visit his aunt.

The breeze makes a muted roaring. Jamel would like to peer down over the edge but is prevented from doing so by a formidable security fence. "So won't nobody try to jump," he points out to Shanice and whoever else might be listening. While she sits on a bench to feed the baby, he wanders off to take in the view, and to work up the nerve to ask his question.

Except for stretches of dull blue-gray water, almost everywhere he looks the earth is covered with a carpet of asphalt, brick, and stone. To the south, freighters slide across New York harbor, heading out into the ocean. To the west, meandering waterways divide the industrial flatlands of New Jersey. North, in the humid haze of late afternoon, midtown bristles with skyscrapers, like the setting for the most advanced level of a video game.

Beneath the rustling of the wind, other sounds emerge: an electrical buzzing, distant traffic noises, passing planes, all distilled down to a mysterious city hum. As Jamel moves around the deck, some of the camera-bearing tourists glance up sharply—a *What might this kid try to grab?* look—but most of them ignore him. They're too busy with their own lives: couples smooching, families posing for pictures. Everyone seems so connected, so part of something. He slips through the crowds feeling like a ghost.

It's a relief when Shanice tugs at his elbow. He looks down at their baby slung in the crook of her arm and bends to kiss Tisha's warm cheek.

"What's that?" Shanice asks, pointing down at the East River.

"Yo, a prison island. Like Alcatraz. I bet it be Rikers."

"Can you see where your house at?" Shanice says.

"Naw, but I see yours." He points across the river to the tiny brown clump of the Wysocki Houses rising from the Brooklyn plains.

A big digital sign on a neighboring building says that it's ninety-two degrees out, but up here it feels cooler, especially as the afternoon shifts into dusk. The spire of the Chrysler Building lights up, and every time Jamel moves close to the railings, he sees more and more lights below: strings of bulbs like Christmas ornaments strung along the bridges, streams of red taillights flowing uptown, yellow headlights flowing down. Shanice murmurs in her daughter's ear as she points out the lit torch of the Statue of Liberty.

"You know what happen if you th'ow a penny offa here?" Jamel says.

"What?"

"It drop right through someone's head." He reaches into his pocket and comes up with a jingle of change.

"*Jamel.*"

"Psych," he says, dropping the change back into his pocket.

Shanice sets Tisha down and she totters toward Jamel, arms held up high. He swings her against his chest. His daughter. She plants a little tickle of a kiss against his cheek, sending a warm electric charge direct to his heart. She's getting heavier every day, but it seems like a weight he's actually happy to carry.

"Yo, Shannie," he says to Shanice.

"Yo, what?"

Jamel sits down. "I wanna aks you somethin'. You know how my house is all big and shit, 'specially since it's just me and my moms?"

Shanice, busy searching through the baby bag for something, doesn't seem to have taken in the question.

"I was thinkin'," Jamel continues, "what about if you and Tisha moved in with me?"

He has her attention now. "You for real?"

"Yeah, baby." The idea was actually his moms'—she likes the idea of being a full-time grandmother—but he's getting interested in the notion himself. Maybe he can get out of this weird limbo he's in, somewhere between single and married. Move forward with his life. "What you think?" he says.

"Don't know," Shanice says, but she's smiling.

"You wanna think about it?"

"I guess." No quips, no barbs.

"Well, while you thinkin' 'bout it, we best go back."

Jamel stands. He's ready to lead his family back to Brooklyn.

CHAPTER TWENTY-SEVEN

"Look," Mitchell says, "let's at least just shut the window."

He gets out of bed, pads over to the front of the house, and peers down at the street. Next door, the big orange cat sits scowling out by the curb. From two doors over, the rap music pounds away. Mitchell tugs his sweaty boxer shorts away from his crotch and grimaces.

"I need fresh air," Kristin says. She's sitting up in bed wearing a silky slip; she looks tired, not as cool and composed as usual.

"Why don't we just turn the air-conditioning on for half an hour and cool things off?" Mitchell asks.

"It's not that hot. And besides, the air-conditioning dries me up."

Mitchell groans. They've been having this argument all summer. His wife needs her precious fresh air, while he'd be happy to just crank up the air-con and let it blast all season long. "Come on," he says. "It'll be quieter in here."

Kristin leans over and takes a sip from a water glass on her bedside table. "It's not so loud this evening."

"Not so loud? It's killing all the goddamn plants outside."

She laughs.

He turns away from the window. "It's not funny. I can't stand this crap."

She adjusts the straps of her slip. "Why do you let the music bother you so much?"

"I don't 'let it.' I don't have any choice. And besides, it's not music—it's just *noise*."

She laughs again.

He returns to sit heavily on the end of the bed. "What's so funny?"

"You sound exactly like my father complaining about rock music. And his father too, probably, complaining about, I don't know . . . *Benny Goodman*."

"It's not the same."

"Why not? We're just getting older. Some new art form comes along and it's hard to understand."

"It's not the same. Rock 'n' roll may have been kind of dumb sometimes, but it had a lot more going for it."

"Oh yeah, like what? *Doo wah diddy*?"

He twists around. "Okay, so maybe some of the lyrics were stupid, but it still had more to it. I mean—look, there's all these different elements in music: you've got rhythm, okay, and melody and harmony. You got all these things going on, and this is what makes it so great. I don't see how it's supposed to be some big creative advance that these guys strip away everything and just leave us with somebody griping away over a drum machine. And then even they realize how *nothing* it is, so they steal stuff off records by real musicians."

She raises her eyebrows. "It sounds like you've been giving this a lot of thought."

"Are you kidding? What else can I think about? I get any other thought in my head and the noise just pounds it out. It's anti-thinking music. And I'll tell you another thing: music is great because it can express all these different emotions like love, sadness, happiness . . . whatever. A lot of different colors. And this gangster rap shit just strips it down to one. Maybe two. They can shout how angry they are, or they can brag about how they've got the most money, or guns, or 'bitches' or something. It's all 'niggers this,' and 'niggers that.'"

"That sounds a little racist."

"*I'm* not the one who says 'niggers.' They do it themselves."

"It still sounds a little racist."

"*Racist?* No way. I'd be the first to say that black people have been the heart of American music. I mean, jazz, blues, soul, all that stuff. I appreciate black music as much as anybody."

He pauses to listen to the bass pounding through the windows, through the brick. He finds a balled-up sock next to the bed and hurls it at the wall. "This is a hot new art form? Have you ever noticed that when they do this stuff live they have to have dancers bouncing all over the stage to cover up the fact that it's so goddamn boring? This isn't music—it's just people who're too untalented to actually make music, shouting."

"That's a huge generalization." Kristin gets up out of bed. "I have to pee." She goes into the bathroom.

"I'm not racist," Mitchell calls out. "I don't like heavy metal, either."

A minute later, his wife returns and climbs back into bed. "I'm sure that there's some good rap music if you know where to look, just like there's gotta be some good heavy metal."

He groans. "Why do you always disagree with me? It's not like you listen to a lot of Snoopy Dog Dog yourself."

"I'm just playing devil's advocate."

"*Why?*"

"Why what?"

He pushes himself up from the bed. "What's the point of doing that? Why not try agreeing with me sometime? Why do you always have to put down what I'm saying? You sound like your mother."

His wife falls back against her pillows with a stricken look on her face. Her eyes well up with tears.

"Kristin?"

She doesn't answer, just covers her face with her hands.

Mitchell stands confused for a moment, then sits down and slides toward her along the bed. "Honey?" He reaches out to her, but she twists away. "Sweetie, what is it?"

She flips onto her stomach and presses her face into the mattress, weeping.

Tentative, he smooths his hand over her shoulder blade. "Honey, I'm sorry. What's the matter?" He leans over and envelops her in his arms. "Kristin? Talk to me. Was it what I said about your mother?"

Sniffing, his wife nods. She sits up, wiping her face, and reaches over to the bedside table for a tissue. She blows her nose loudly.

He winces. "Why did you react so, uh, *strongly* to what I said?"

She chews her lip. "It just . . . it *hurt*."

He waits patiently.

She snuffles again. "I've been talking to Dr. Simon about my mother recently."

"Here," Mitchell says, handing her the water glass. He smooths a soggy strand of blond hair off her cheek. While she sips the water, he surreptitiously licks his finger, tasting the salt from her tears.

She lies back. He scoots up behind her and wraps his arms around her stomach. She loosens his grip. He takes offense, until she says that it's just because she feels bloated.

"What about your mother?" he says.

She lies still. He barely breathes, afraid to disturb her train of thought. Finally, she sighs. "Am I mean to you?"

"No, honey, of course not."

She turns over to face him. "Be honest with me, Mitchell."

He blinks, considering what he can say that won't get him into more trouble, or be held against him in some future argument. "Why do you ask?" he says, buying time.

Her eyes water again. "Sometimes I hear myself and I'm afraid that I *am* sounding just like her. The way she always put my father down. Do you think I do that to you?"

He sighs. "I just wish . . . I wish you'd try a little harder to see my side of things sometimes. Like this noise business. It's not my fault that we're having this problem. You know?"

She winces. "I'm sorry, honey. I'll try to be more understanding. Okay?"

A wave of tenderness sweeps over Mitchell. He leans down and kisses his wife. After a moment, he cups her breast and gathers up the hem of her slip.

Later, after the sweat is drying on their skin, Mitchell turns to find that his wife has drifted into sleep. He lies back, relaxed finally, musing on the unpredictable twists and turns of marriage.

* * *

A few evenings later, he meets his wife and two of her friends in an old tin-ceilinged bar in Soho. Pamela, an anorexic-looking blonde wearing a dress made out of some sort of metallic fabric, is a co-worker at Kristin's bridal magazine. Her husband Alan, with his Caesar haircut and long sideburns, is evidently involved in some sort of Internet P.R. work, but Mitchell does not feel the energy or inclination to find out what. He looks across the table at his wife, who is listening to her colleague go on about some upcoming home furnishings show. She seems unusually cheerful, and he wonders why.

At a neighboring table, two young women sip mineral water and wave their hands about as they chatter away in Italian. One of them—flowing hennaed hair, gaunt cheekbones, nipples visible through her black T-shirt—notices Michael's surreptitious gaze and smiles a stunning red-lipped smile. He turns to see if Kristin saw, but she's gossiping blithely with her friends.

When a waiter comes to take their order, Alan and Pamela order wine and Mitchell asks for a Scotch, but Kristin just orders a Perrier.

"Aren't you going to have a real drink?" Pamela asks.

"Well . . ." Kristin says, blushing. "I can't."

"What do you mean?" says Pamela.

Kristin turns to Mitchell. "I'm sorry, honey—I wanted to tell you later, as a surprise, but I went to the doctor today and . . . I'm pregnant."

She starts to cry. And then Pamela starts to cry.

Mitchell can only say, "You're what?! How?"

Alan says, "Didn't they explain that to you in fifth grade gym class?"

Mitchell is momentarily struck dumb.

"Aren't you pleased?" asks Pamela.

"Of course," he recovers, and reaches across the table to grasp his wife's hands. As he looks into her flushed, luminous face, he tries to sort through the welter of emotions surging in his chest. One predominates: relief. Relief that she is fertile, yes, and relief that he is potent, but more than that, it's relief that after so many years of confusion and frustration, things might finally be turning around. He is not doomed to be an observer of life passing him by, not a victim of muggers or his father's mistakes or anything else. He has started a family, and he will get his promotion. If he wants to, he'll open a restaurant.

He grins at his wife. "Yes, I am. I'm really happy."

CHAPTER TWENTY-EIGHT

"Look out!" Charles Matthews calls from above.

Grace stands on her dark fire escape, tensing as a bottle rocket comes whizzing over the edge of the roof.

"Damn kids," Charles mutters, but they both laugh.

"I'm going to hand up the bread pudding now." Grace stands on tiptoe, holding up a heavy baking pan as Charles, an indistinct form in the darkness, reaches down over the ladder.

"Okay, now the chairs."

She passes up a couple of folding beach chairs.

"Don't forget the port," he adds. "And the glasses."

She hands up a basket containing the last items for their Fourth of July picnic, then gingerly climbs the rusty iron ladder herself, careful not to look down as she goes. Charles's strong hand clamps to her arm to help her over the lip of the roof.

"I can't believe you never come up here," he says. "The view is tremendous."

She stands, breathing in the warm night air. Beyond the dark shape of a chimney and the front edge of the roof, a streetlight makes a halo through a cloud of summer leaves. The evening is young, but already firecrackers are snapping all around. In the distance the skyline of Manhattan glows like a luminous honeycomb.

"Your tar beach," Charles says with satisfaction, surveying the roof. "A true Brooklyn phenomenon."

"Have you been on one before?"

He smiles. "No. Where I come from, we had real beaches."

"Me too," she says, and thinks back, not of beaches, but of sitting on a front porch inhaling the scent of flowers in the night: jacaranda, bougainvillea, ginger plant—

"Ohh, look!" he exclaims.

She turns. "What is it?"

"Keep looking."

Above Park Slope a firework dandelion puffs open, shimmers, and fades. Grace turns slowly; far off over Bay Ridge, over Carroll Gardens, even over Staten Island and New Jersey, tiny fireworks blossom in the night.

She bends down. It's hard to see in the darkness, but she manages to spoon up two servings of her bread pudding. Charles busies himself preparing the port.

"To us," he says, and hands her a glass.

The chairs creak as they settle down. Charles digs into his pudding with gusto, sighing to show his appreciation.

Such a sweet man, she thinks. He knows how unhappy and distracted she has been these past weeks, so he has dreamed up this picnic to take her mind off things. Lord knows she needs a change: she has been like a compost heap burning with a slow internal fire. Tonight she's going to forget about her non-promotion, forget about the noise problem in the courtyard, forget about what she has been thinking of doing recently . . . She sips the sweet wine and smiles; his plan seems to be working. They'll enjoy the night air for a while, and then descend the ladder, and undoubtedly they'll make love. Almost better, even, they'll make small talk as they undress, and joke with each other while they brush their teeth, and she'll wrap her arms around him as they settle in for sleep.

As the evening tips into night, the rattling of firecrackers takes on a frenzied pace. Two streets over, an aerial firework explodes over the roofs with a dazzling brilliance. Several roofs away, another bottle rocket screams up . . . BANG!

As Grace is about to suggest that they retreat from the roof, shouts and a smashing noise rise up from the street. Charles stands and walks over to the front edge.

"Please be careful," she calls. Another crash from the street. Moved by curiosity, she edges to the lip of the roof. Down below, two black teenagers are rummaging in a recycling barrel. One of them straightens up and cocks his arm.

Across the street a third youth ducks behind a car as a bottle smashes on a fence. "Cocksackie motherfucker!" he shouts and hurls some projectile back, which cracks the side window of one of the cars parked along the street.

Hooting with laughter, the boys run around the corner toward the projects.

"Should we call the police?" Charles says.

"It wouldn't do any good now. They're gone." Grace bends to pack the plates and glasses into the basket.

Charles pauses in the middle of folding up the chairs. "Grace—"

"Yes?"

"Don't you think of moving away from here?"

"Just because of a few boys getting out of hand on the Fourth of July?"

"You know what I mean."

She does. She thinks of Jeeps cruising menacingly by, of hooded teenagers checking their beepers next to the pay phone around the corner. It's strange to think of mere children holding such sway, not because of any real authority, but simply because they're able to buy guns.

"In my day," Charles says, "those boys would never have gotten away with what they just did. There would have been neighbors looking out who knew them, and those neighbors would've disciplined them just as if they had been their own."

"Nobody wants to discipline a child who might be carrying a gun."

"Well, that's what I mean. These kids have no respect. They don't want to work, they just want fast money, easy money."

Grace bends to crimp tin foil over the baking pan. So far, she and Charles have not had a serious argument about anything. She sighs. "What kind of jobs do you think they could get, coming from those projects?"

Charles lifts the chairs over the top of the ladder. "They can start out at the bottom, like I did. It doesn't kill anyone to deliver a few newspapers or do a little factory work."

She nests the baking pan in the basket. "And then what? How are they going to move up, with no education to speak of?"

"If there's a will, a way can be found," he replies. She hears a peevish tone entering his voice, as if she's questioning his own hard-earned success.

She watches him descend the ladder, then hands down the basket and makes her own way down.

"The world has changed," she says as she climbs in through the kitchen window. "Even if the will and the education are there, the work isn't. Almost all of the factory jobs are gone around here. What do these kids know about computers or office work?" She sets the basket on the table and moves to the sink to fill the teapot.

Charles frowns. "Making excuses for this behavior can only harm our people. There has to come a point when you say This is right, that's wrong. We have to take responsibility for our behavior."

Let it go, says a little voice in her head, but her anger begins to surface. "You think this is a moral issue? Do you honestly think little babies make a decision to grow up in that place? Why would you expect that—living in that situation—those boys would miraculously come up with middle-class ideas about personal responsibility and choice? If you . . . if I plant a seed, and then give it hardly any water or sunlight, should I get mad at it because it doesn't grow into a tree?"

He grimaces. "Listen, Grace, it's late. Why don't we just change the subject?"

Maybe it's her exasperation with his tone, or her desire to unburden herself—she's not sure which, but she sits at the kitchen table and gravely confronts him. "Charles, there's something I want to tell you."

A flicker of fear passes over his face. He sits too. "What is it? Are you okay?"

"I'm okay. I'm . . . not okay. I mean, I'm fine healthwise and all, but I've been thinking about what happened to me at the Beardon Group."

Charles waits to see where this may be headed.

Grace gets up again and busies herself with the tea. She takes a deep breath, then turns to him. "I've been thinking about filing a discrimination complaint with the Equal Opportunity Commission."

He sits there looking as if she's just punched him in the back of the head. "You . . . how can you . . . I mean how do you know that—"

"Look, I've thought it over from every angle. There's no other explanation for what happened to me. Edward Laidlaw even admitted it to my face."

"But you don't have proof. It would be his word against yours."

"I don't know if I need proof. The question is, how else can they justify what they did to me?"

"If this got ugly, Grace, and I imagine it would, they'd make a huge effort to dig up any past problem or impropriety—"

She chuckles bitterly. "Listen to me, Charles: there *were* no improprieties. In thirty-five years, I've done everything strictly by the book. I never padded an expense account, rarely even took a sick day, never did a single thing I'd be embarrassed to admit in court. That's what makes this so crazy—I've been a perfect employee."

Charles kneads his hands together. Outside, the fireworks have risen to a continuous clattering rumble.

"Have you thought about the consequences of this, Grace?"

"Of course I have. I've been worried about the effect on my co-workers if there's bad publicity for the company, but I don't think I'd be doing them any favors by remaining silent. If I don't do anything, maybe someday the company will do something like this to them. To tell the truth, the only thing I'm really worried about is the effect this might have on you, as a member of the board and everything."

Charles sighs deeply. "I don't think you should worry about me." He stares out toward the garden. "I don't know what to think."

They sit in a troubled silence for several minutes. Finally, Grace makes an effort to salvage the evening. She forces herself to keep her tone light. "Will you stay tonight, Charles?"

He clinks his teaspoon around the inside of the cup. "I'm feeling very tired. If you don't mind, I think I'll just call a car and go home."

She nods glumly.

He picks up the phone.

* * *

Thankfully, the car arrives in five minutes, sparing them further inability to speak. After a perfunctory kiss at the front door, Charles trudges out.

Grace washes the dessert plates, her mind a jumble. She feels ashamed for lecturing Charles on the poverty in the projects. Should she have obeyed her instincts and changed the subject earlier? Should she have waited for some other moment to bring up the EEOC complaint? But what is their relationship worth if she can't tell him what's in her heart?

She lifts her cup to her lips, but the tea has grown cold.

She pictures Charles riding home in the back seat of the car; remembers the first time she saw his apartment, with its one pair of boots in the hall, its one lone toothbrush by the bathroom sink.

Half an hour later, she lies in bed, weary, so weary, wishing to be free of the bitter, obsessive voice unspooling in her head—free of her anger at Edward Laidlaw, of her guilt at turning Carol Fasone away so sharply, of arguments about race and responsibility, of worrying about what she should or shouldn't have said. To go back to a time before she didn't get her promotion, a time before the ceaseless noise out in the courtyard, a time when she could go quietly about her work and then come home and have a peaceful cup of tea in the garden.

But not a time before Charles. She wants to lie in bed, to look at a warm rectangle of light in the bathroom doorway, to listen to the humming inside, to know that in just a moment he'll emerge from that door and come and slip under the sheets beside her.

She stares up at the dark ceiling, hugging herself in fear.

CHAPTER TWENTY-NINE

CAROL WAITS, AS SHE HAS WAITED ALL DAY FOR THE PAST TWO DAYS, in a secluded corner of the plaza, not daring to leave even to get food, in case she misses Milosz striding in to class.

One bench down, two lovers twine around each other. The young man whispers into his girl's ear, and she twists her neck, big gold earrings jangling, and nuzzles up to him. They seem oblivious to the world around them—certainly oblivious to Carol sitting just five feet away. When the girl leans back onto the boy's lap and he bends down to engage her in a soulful open-mouthed kiss, Carol discreetly moves to another bench.

She waits. A teen rollerblader sluices by, zipping in and out of the row of benches. Several benches down, a dreadlocked young man submerged in the private concert in his earphones lets out an occasional high moan of vocal support, an unconscious *Ooeee!* or *Unhunh!* that elicits grins of amusement from the passersby.

Out in the sun-baked center of the plaza, pigeons bob around a scattering of bread crumbs, scarcely bothering to move out of the way of the constant flow of pedestrian traffic. And there, far across the way, comes a lone figure with a familiar cocky strut. She's not quite sure it's Milosz, but he stops to light a cigarette and by the characteristic tilt of his head she knows him. She almost shouts, but voices are easily lost in this vast open space—and besides, she retains enough presence of mind to recognize the advantage of surprise.

As she watches him approach, ambling along as if he doesn't have a worry in the world, her chest constricts and her eyes narrow. He doesn't care, she realizes. He simply does not care. In order to do what he's done, there could be no room in his bony chest for love of her. Why should there be room in her heart for forgiveness?

She waits until he's ten yards from the front entrance before she jumps up and runs forward.

"Milosz!"

He turns, his questioning look giving way to an unguarded instant of stupefaction, perhaps even fear. With a pang, she notices that his face looks even more gaunt than before. He darts toward the entrance.

"Milosz!" she calls again, and reaches the glass doors a moment after he slips through. She lunges across the lobby, almost slipping on the freshly washed marble floor—there he is standing next to an elevator bank, *trapped*—but she is stopped by a security guard who rises from behind a desk.

"Excuse me, ma'am, I need to see your I.D."

Beyond the checkpoint, Milosz stares at her like a cornered fox.

"Ma'am? Are you with the college?"

"No, I . . . *that man*." She points, breathless. "He's my husband."

The guard turns to Milosz, who does not say anything. An elevator door slides open, he gives a furtive glance back, then disappears.

CHAPTER THIRTY

THE NEXT WEEKEND, MITCHELL CARRIES A PLATE OF TOAST OUT
TO the garden, walking almost on tiptoe, as if he can magically preserve the sunlit hush of the court. His optimism is not completely
unfounded: the night before, though Friday, had been mysteriously,
blissfully silent. Perhaps, he thinks, the Wilson kid got arrested for
some other obnoxiousness and there will finally be peace on the block.
Or maybe the jerk finally decided he was a grown-up and—wanting
to be free of his mother, who must be no treat to live with—went off
to party elsewhere, someplace where he can torment a new bunch of
neighbors.

The day is hot but still, with only a couple of small clouds gliding
gracefully across the deep blue sky. Mitchell returns to the kitchen
for a Bloody Mary. Nine-thirty, reads the clock over the stove. Still
quiet.

Sitting at the picnic table outside, waiting for his wife to get home
from a shopping expedition, he stirs the glass to evenly distribute
the flecks of horseradish through the red. Soon the sun will be too
high and too strong, starching the life out of lawns that have already
gone weeks without rain, but for now he can sit and read the *Times*
in peace—at least, when he's not obsessing about his impending
fatherhood.

He looks over his shoulder: the Wilsons' back door is open, but
the yard is empty except for their gray, unhealthy-looking dog, which
trots restlessly about, poking its head into the corners.

Mitchell butters a slice of toast and props the sports section open on the table. He crunches into his breakfast. As if by bad magic, at that exact second the music blasts out across the empty court: the heavy bass beats slam and echo against the houses across the way.

Mitchell resolves that—by force of will—he's simply going to ignore the noise and read his paper. Two minutes later, unable to focus on any article and wilting under the steady barrage, he groans and crumples the paper into a ball. He stands and crosses to the fence, staring helplessly at the Wilsons' yard.

"Hello!" he calls. "Turn it down!"

He might as well be shouting under a Boeing 747.

Cursing, he gathers up his breakfast and carries it inside. When he was buying the house, he and Kristin talked excitedly about all the barbecues and dinner parties they'd have in the garden, lighting the walkway with candle-bright paper bags, but they haven't had a single gathering in the past month for fear it would be spoiled by the noise.

Inside his house, too riled up to eat, he paces between the back and front windows, peering out for signs of the Wilsons. He's tempted to get the phone chain going, but nervous that the music might spontaneously stop before the cops show up. *If* they show up. The last time he called, they said they couldn't do much if the noise wasn't happening after eleven at night—though why it should be okay to ruin other people's lives during the day is not at all clear.

He decides to give it another half hour and see if the music doesn't stop by then. And it does.

He makes some more toast and drinks another Bloody Mary. Feeling logy, he crawls back to bed for a nap, promising himself he'll get a jump on some office work when he wakes.

At four o'clock, the courtyard is silent and he should be calm, but—after his nap and several hours of procrastination—he boots up his computer to find that, for some mysterious reason, his new work file won't open. He searches through the Help manual twice without luck and ends up on the phone, on hold, waiting to get through on the 1-800 support line, forced to listen to a Muzak version of Barry Manilow's "Copacabana." After ten minutes, he starts to get anxious—he promised Mr. Reincke he'd help put together a big report for the Monday meeting.

Outside, the music starts up again, but at an unusually low volume. Cradling the receiver in the crook of his neck, he picks up the phone and carries it to the kitchen window. To his horror, the Wilson yard is abuzz with activity. Through the intervening vines and bushes, he sees the kid doing something to a barbecue grill while a couple of his friends have a pretend boxing match. An orange-haired girl looks on as a baby toddles around the yard. Mrs. Wilson pulls picnic supplies out of some shopping bags—judging by the number of buns and other items, they're preparing for a humongous barbecue.

* * *

"Baby, I hope you cleaned up your room."

Jamel turns to his mother, sighs, and drops his head back in disgust. "I aksed you not to call me that."

She ignores this comment. "Your room?"

"Won't nobody be lookin' in my room."

"*Jamel.*"

He rolls his eyes and heads back into the house. No point in upsetting his mother after she agreed to this party, this celebration of the dropping of the charges against Tree. (At first it appeared that his friend would have to do some time, but Tree's drug dealer boss agreed to testify against his suppliers, and the lesser charges facing his minions were dropped). His mother had been reluctant to host a party at first, telling Jamel he could only have a few close friends over, but then she started inviting some of her friends, and soon the guest list mushroomed.

In his room, he picks some clothes off the floor and tosses them in a closet. He takes a minute to do an excellent job of making his bed—Who knows, maybe he'll be able to persuade Shanice to sneak up here for a few minutes when the party gets busy. Can't hurt to hope. He takes a long shower, absorbed in this fantasy. Maybe today she'll announce that she has agreed to move in.

It's only four-thirty, but he gets dressed for the party anyhow, taking special pride in his clean Air Jordans and a new Hilfiger shirt he bought in a moment of weakness when he should have been saving the money from his jobs.

He comes downstairs to find Onica in the kitchen. She grins and kisses him on the cheek. It's good to see her looking happy; ever since Tree got busted, she's been so miserable and nervous that he has been worried about her. She stirs barbecue sauce into an aluminum pan full of chicken. Her hands are conspicuously free of jewelry—she sold her engagement ring to hire Tree a lawyer, instead of leaving him in the hands of one of the overburdened public defenders.

Downstairs, Jamel stands in the back doorway and watches Shanice set out paper plates on the picnic table. Their daughter walks in quick tottery steps around the yard.

"Come to Daddy, girl."

Tisha stares across the lawn at him and abruptly collapses onto her bottom. She doesn't cry, though, just extends a chubby hand and grabs a fistful of dry grass. He steps out across the yard and scoops her up. She laughs as he swings her up in the air.

"Who's my little girl?" he says. "Is it Tisha?"

"Papa," she says. "Papa."

He sets her down and holds her hand as she wanders around the garden. He loves the grip of her tiny fingers.

"Jamel!"

He rolls his eyes and looks up at his mother in the kitchen window. She holds out some money.

"They'll deliver the keg, but we gonna need a lot of ice to chill it down. Get about eight of them big bags, if you can carry it."

* * *

Late in the afternoon Grace stands in her kitchen, gazing out at her garden. She has done her best to keep it watered, but the weeks of sun have taken a toll. The grass looks wilted, and the roses are brown at the edges.

She looks toward the silent phone. She hasn't spoken to Charles Matthews in almost five days.

She thinks. All day long, she hasn't done much else. A little shopping for necessities, a little cleaning, but really she's been turned inward, monitoring her deepest thoughts and feelings.

Now something finally comes together. She finishes a glass of iced tea, then goes out into the hall, finds her briefcase, and takes out a blank legal pad.

Back at the kitchen table, she sits down, pen in hand, and begins to write.

I first came to work at the Beardon Group (at that time called the Beardon Insurance Company), on September 7, 1970. I started work as a secretary in the accounting department. My responsibilities included: taking dictation, filing, and

She stops, then returns to the top of the page, where she writes in her perfect handwriting:

To: the Equal Employment Opportunity Commission

She pauses again, awed by this first step. From outside, Jamel Wilson's music thumps through the window, echoing her own beating heart. She thinks of a Sunday school lecture when she was a little girl, Joshua and his trumpet calling down the walls of Jericho. She knows that she may be trumpeting down her own walls as well, but perhaps this isn't such a bad thing. Maybe she can find a way to live beyond the walls.

She writes.

* * *

Across the way, Carol washes a sinkful of dishes, grinning to herself as she recalls the previous afternoon.

"So, whaddaya think?" Tom McGlynn had said as he got out of his car in front of her house.

Carol inspected her co-worker and nodded enthusiastically.

McGlynn grinned broadly. He looked very official in his best work suit, with a little metal flag pinned to his lapel, with his mirrored sunglasses. "Wait—you gotta get the full effect." He reached into his pocket and pulled out a single earphone on a wire.

She had laughed. "It's perfect. Thanks for taking the afternoon off for me."

"No sweat, Fasone. This is gonna be my pleasure." He gestured at a Lincoln Town Car double-parked at the curb. Inside, another beefy man, younger but similarly attired, waved at Carol.

"My cousin Eddie," McGlynn said. "He always wanted to be an actor."

The cousin shifted to the back seat and they drove along Smith Street towards the Fulton Mall. The funny thing was, during the ride McGlynn didn't crack a single joke. He talked about how he spent weekends on his pride and joy, a small fishing boat he kept docked out at Sheepshead Bay. At work there was often something forced and anxious about him, but now he was calm and relaxed. He seemed, in fact, like a nice guy. Carol glanced over at him in the passenger seat, sitting there nodding his head contentedly in time with the radio. She didn't feel the electrical charge she always got in Milosz's presence, but a lot of that charge—she realized now—was based on nervousness, on trying to figure out how to please her husband, on being continually off base. With McGlynn she didn't have to worry about whether she said the right thing, whether she might inadvertently send him into a mood. She couldn't exactly picture him making passionate love on the kitchen table, but then again, she could picture him doing something Milosz might have been incapable of: making a little kid laugh.

Soon the three of them were standing under an arcade next to the Technical College. Every few seconds Carol peered around a column to scan the broad plaza.

Five minutes later her heart skipped a beat. "Here he comes."

"The one with the orange knapsack?" asked McGlynn.

"No, the guy with the Popeye walk—over there."

"Not a bad lookin' fella," her co-worker said grudgingly.

"Get going! You have to catch him before he gets inside." Her heart hammered as she watched McGlynn and his cousin step out onto the

plaza. He turned and offered a quick thumbs-up, and then they trot-
ted forward.

"Excuse me!" He called out toward the distant figure. "Excuse
me—sir?"

Carol ducked back until she was almost completely hidden.

Milosz turned warily as the two business-suited men jogged up,
one on each side. McGlynn flashed his wallet and the fake I.D. he
had made on his home computer. Carol wished she were closer so she
could see the look on her husband's face as he was confronted by the
"Immigration and Naturalization Service officers." She wished she
could ride along as they drove him out to the airport; could listen as
they announced that they were going to immediately put him on a
plane out of the country; could watch his stricken face as they took
him up to a ticket counter, told him to wait on line, and then left him
standing there.

(Despite the exhortations of her fellow secretaries, she didn't have
it in her to get him deported for real, but that didn't mean she would
let him off without feeling at least a tiny bit of the pain he had put her
through.)

When she told her mother about it later, the old woman laughed so
hard she nearly choked on a piece of steak.

* * *

By seven the party is in full swing. The barbecue is fired up; Jamel
flips hamburgers and chicken, his face averted from the smoke siz-
zling up off the grill. Tree, sheepish at finding himself the center of
attention, sits on a red vinyl couch in the corner of the yard while his
friends quiz him about his time in the House of Detention.

"I hope you didn't drop no soap when you was in them showers,"
says one squat kid wearing a Phillies sweatshirt.

"*Shee*," Tree says. "All a them niggahs knew whose crew I was
wit', so din't nobody mess."

The speaker cabinets in the basement are propped up to play out
into the yard.

By nine o'clock word of the party has spread far and wide, drawing such local dignitaries as Tee-Ali and his crew from the projects. Jamel takes them down in the basement, where they can share a blunt.

After a few minutes Shanice's gangly little sister Michelle comes running breathless down the front steps from outside.

"Git outta here, girl," Jamel says.

"Th-the police outside."

"So?" Jamel crosses over to the sound mixer and lowers the volume. "Wait up, y'all." He climbs the steps to the front stoop.

Out in the street sits a police cruiser, lights flashing.

Jamel pushes open the gate and bends down to speak into the open front window. "What's the problem, officer?"

"You live here, son?" asks the cop in the passenger seat.

"We just having a birthday party, that's all."

"We've had a couple of calls at the precinct about the noise levels. Would you mind lowering the stereo a couple of notches?"

"No problem, sir."

The cop nods. The radio crackles with another call and the car pulls away. Jamel turns to find his mother standing on the front stoop with her arms crossed.

"Don't you worry about it," she says. "We pay our mortgage just like anybody else. They ain't driving us outta here—we got a right to have a little party."

Jamel descends to the basement and pushes the volume up again. He turns the front pair of speakers away from the storm door so that the volume in front of the house won't seem so loud. "Let's get somethin' to eat," he says to Tee-Ali and company.

In the backyard, torches on tall bamboo poles flicker in the darkness. Smoke hisses up as Tree dumps another pan of chicken on the grill. Clumps of friends and relatives sit on folding chairs around the yard: in this corner Jamel's aunt Simone is talking to her daughter Jackie and her son-in-law Dennis; over there Onica's mother CeeCee bounces a baby on her lap while Shanice stoops to grab Tisha, who's climbing up on the picnic table. "I gotta be watching her all the time," Shanice tells CeeCee. "She always opening cabinets, goin' up stairs . . ."

"Where's that West Indian woman I seen across the yard the last time I was over?" CeeCee asks Jamel's mother.

Melba snorts. "That gal think she too good for people like us. Too yellah."

She gestures to Jamel to turn the music down, and then she and Onica go inside and return with a big frosted cake topped with some leftover Fourth of July sparklers. Onica cries as they present the cake to Tree, who stands there awkwardly, scratching the side of his mouth in embarrassment. Melba beams with pride at seeing her friends and relatives all gathered together in her yard. Everybody cheers as Tree scoops off a corner of the cake and takes a bite. Then Jamel descends into the basement and cranks up the stereo.

Soon the basement fills with sweaty dancers and sweet clouds of pot smoke. He puts on a slow song so he can dance with Shanice. As they turn languidly, heads sunk on each other's shoulders, he feels a tug on his pants leg and looks down to see his daughter staring up. Tisha, shy all of a sudden, scoots off through a sea of slowly turning adults. Jamel turns to Shanice and they exchange a deep kiss.

* * *

At ten-thirty Carol lies in bed, sleeping. The loud music from across the court continues, but she has finally managed to drift off.

She's having a flying dream: she's in a street somewhere, one of the stone canyons near work, and people in business suits stare up at her as she swoops by overhead.

* * *

At eleven-thirty Grace, tense and unable to sleep, pads down to her kitchen for a cup of tea. While she waits for the water to boil, she glances out the window at the Wilson's yard, a bustle of figures moving in and out of the flickering light. Despite her notion that the boy should be able to play his music unhindered, this late-night volume is clearly overstepping the bounds.

She lifts the teapot off the stove and is filling her cup when the phone rings. She expects it's one of the neighbors, calling to try once more to enlist her in their phone chain. She lets it ring five or six times, but finally picks up.

"It's me."

She sits, hardly breathing.

"I'm sorry to wake you."

"No, Charles, I wasn't sleeping."

"You weren't? Me neither. I mean, I suppose that's obvious, seeing as how I'm calling you . . . Listen," he says gravely, "I've been wanting to talk to you."

"You have?" she says, feeling her throat clamp up. She grips the arms of her chair, steeling herself.

"About the other night—"

"Yes?"

"Grace, I'm sorry."

"You are?"

"I don't know what happened," he says. "I guess I was tired and a little grumpy—"

"*I* was grumpy," she says. Her hands loosen their grip.

"Anyhow, since I haven't heard from you for the last several days, I thought maybe you were mad at me."

She laughs in relief.

"What's so funny?"

"Nothing."

"Listen, Grace, I've been missing you."

"You have?"

"Of course I have."

A smile spreads like warm honey across her face, but then she glances down at the legal pad on her kitchen table. She swallows. "Charles, I've been busy today."

"You have? With what?"

"I wrote a letter to the EEOC."

There's a silence. She almost expects him to hang up.

"Charles?"

"I'm here."

"What do you think?"

He sighs a long sigh. "Grace, I've been thinking about my marriage a lot this week."

Her face falls. "You have? What about it?"

"I've been thinking that my wife never meant as much to me as you do. Never. I've been thinking that I don't care what you do about the Beardon Group, as long as you're sure it's the right thing. I mean, I care—but I don't care about my position on the board. You mean a lot more to me."

A moment of silence.

"Grace?"

"I'm here," she says. "I'm here."

* * *

At two in the morning, after the third time the police have come, the third time the kid has turned the music down only to crank it up again a moment later, Mitchell rises in the blue glow of his bedroom TV, which he has turned to nearly full volume in a futile effort to drown out the noise. (He has already decided that it's useless to try to sleep.) He sets his fourth beer of the evening down on the bedside table, stomps across the house to the back window, and pushes the curtains aside a couple of inches in order to peek out at the party guests gathered in the Wilsons' yard.

"Savages," he says, returning to Kristin, who's sitting up in bed reading a magazine. "They've even got flaming torches."

He plops down on the bed and pulls a pillow over his ears. No help. He throws it against the wall and cracks an eye at the bedside clock. He's going to have to wake early so he can go in to the office and work on the report—whether he gets any sleep or not, the deadline hangs over his head.

"Goddamn *fucker*," he snarls.

The bass pounds against his forehead like a hammer. Anger rises inside of him like uncontrollable bile.

"That's it," he says, rising. "Time to put an end to this bullshit."

"What are you doing?" asks Kristin, looking up from her magazine.

"I'm gonna tell them to turn it down."

"*Mitchell*, please. It's not worth it."

"You're right. It's not worth owning a house and having your life destroyed just so some teenager can amuse himself."

"Mitchell," she calls as he leaves the room and marches down the stairs.

Outside, he stands in the shadow of his front doorway, assessing the situation two doors down. A silver Jeep double-parked in the street gleams under a streetlight, its stereo adding another layer to the din jackhammering out of the basement. A girl jumps out, hollers, and clangs the front gate open to join a group of teenagers milling around the Wilsons' little concrete yard.

Mitchell looks at the houses across the street, wondering about all of the people there. Surely they can't be sleeping through the racket—so why don't they complain? Because they're scared.

He waits a minute until most of the figures in the yard descend into the basement. A lighter flares and a glowing joint is passed around among the small group still standing there. "Yo, shit!" somebody shouts as his buddy drops the roach. One of them moves forward to close the gate: under the light of the streetlamp, Mitchell recognizes Jamel Wilson, with his little joke of a goatee.

A whoop rises from the basement and then, unbelievably, the music booms louder. Inside Mitchell a floodgate opens. Shaking with fury he descends his stoop, yanks open the gate, and marches toward the Wilsons' house.

He stands outside their yard. "That's enough."

Jamel, on his way back to join his friends, turns in surprise. A couple of the other kids look up, but they seem only mildly interested.

"Say what?" Jamel says.

"I said," Mitchell shouts, "*Turn it down*."

"Can't hear you, mister," Jamel replies, cupping his hand behind his ear.

Mitchell is about to shout again when he notices the boy's friends grinning and realizes he's being made an object of fun. One of the youths, a short but menacing kid wearing wrap-around sunglasses under the hood of his sweatshirt, steps forward. "Yo, you best get back home before somebody puts a cap in your ass."

The others cackle, slap each other five.

Mitchell sees a crowd standing on the sidelines, laughing at him after he missed the puck, dropped the ball. Laughing at him in the goldfish bowl.

Ears burning with shame and anger, he retreats down the walk to his house.

Back then, back in high school, there was nothing he could do about the humiliation. But there's something he can do about it now.

* * *

The music and the TV are so loud that Kristin doesn't hear as he bounds down the basement steps two at a time; doesn't hear as he digs out a cardboard box, roots under his old textbooks for the small, heavy bundle wrapped in Tiffany's felt. Hands trembling, he uncovers the gun and inserts the clip. "Just going to scare them," he mutters. "Teach them a little respect."

He trots back up the steps, the weight of the gun in his hand the weight of a tool, like a hammer.

"Mitchell?" Kristin calls from upstairs, but he ignores her and strides out the front door, holding the gun low behind his right leg.

* * *

"Yo shit, white meat coming back for more," calls out the kid with the wraparound shades as Mitchell approaches the Wilson's gate. The kid stands jauntily in front of the open storm doors as the noise thunders up behind him.

Mitchell ignores him and faces Jamel. "Turn the music down."

"We got a right to party in our own damn house."

"I've asked you a number of times, politely, to turn it down."

Tee-Ali takes a step forward. "What he sayin', Richie Cunningham, is we havin' a party and you not invited—so get your sorry ass back home." His buddies double over with laughter.

Mitchell pulls the gun out from behind his leg.

Jamel sees something glint in the man's hand. With a start, he recognizes it and turns to take cover.

Mitchell points the gun away from the teenagers, off toward the sidewalk. Instinctively, he closes his eyes and turns his face away from the sharp sound he's about to uncork. He squeezes his extended hand, surprised by the sharp bark and recoil of the gun. He opens his eyes to see the teenagers cowering in the corner of the yard. He's surprised by how good he feels all of a sudden, no longer at anyone's mercy. Taking action.

* * *

Grace wakes in the middle of the night.

"What is it?" Charles mumbles, rolling over, heavy with sleep. In the dark she can just make out his clothes, lying on the floor for once instead of neatly folded. (He'd joked that after their phone conversation, he nearly jumped into a cab wearing his pajamas.)

"Go back to sleep," she says. "It's probably just some kids from the projects, using up the last of their firecrackers."

* * *

Over by the cellar stairs, the kid with the wraparound shades is reaching into the pocket of his sweatshirt. Pulling something out and lifting it up. A gun.

Panic spurts through Mitchell's veins. He swings his own gun around.

Jamel watches in horror as his daughter's little cornrowed head emerges over the top step from the basement and her tiny hands push down against the concrete.

Mitchell closes his eyes and pumps the trigger, squeezing off several quick rounds.

One bullet shatters the right side of Tisha's head, blowing a puff of red spray across the walk.

Jamel lets out a strangled cry.

Mitchell opens his eyes. He follows the stunned gaze of the teenagers to a small crumpled form on the walk.

For a second, everyone stands frozen.

Then Mitchell backs through the gate, turns, and starts to run.

* * *

Down through the Wilsons' cellar door, sweaty bodies are still swaying to the music. Jamel sits on the cool concrete of the walk, cradling his daughter's limp body. He tries to say her name, but his throat feels like it's filled with slowly drying concrete. He turns to Tee-Ali, swallows, says, "Go down and get my mother."

Tee-Ali descends into the basement and the music abruptly stops. "Yo, whussup with that?" somebody grumbles. Then there's a scream, and Melba runs up out of the basement, followed by Shanice, Onica, and Tree.

* * *

Mitchell runs blindly. A cramp is building in his side but he's too panicked to stop. When he reaches Court Street he hears a faint shout and looks over his shoulder at several figures running toward him, a block behind. Breath ragged in his chest, he quickens his pace.

A couple of men in business suits and loosened neckties come out of a sports bar and jump back as he runs past—he's puzzled until he looks down and sees that he's still holding the gun. He stumbles to the nearest corner and stuffs it into a public trash can, under a greasy Styrofoam takeout container. He wipes his hand on his leg and dodges down a side street. He runs a little slower, knowing that his pursuers didn't see where he went, but the enormity of the trouble he has left behind is so great—a wounded child, another child growing in his wife's belly who'll be traumatized forever by his rash act—that the only way he can keep it from crushing him is to move on.

A siren sounds in the distance. Running steadily, he looks back along the leafy tunnel of the street to see a squad car blink past down Court. At the end of the next block, he bursts out of the dim side street onto Atlantic Avenue: a kissing couple breaks apart to gawk, a blue neon sign glows, a traffic light blinks from green to red. He darts out across the avenue and a horn blares as he's almost hit by a passing truck.

* * *

An ambulance pulls up in front of the Wilson house. Cops push back the crowd while the paramedics examine the little body, but there's no resuscitation to be performed, nothing to be done.

The yard is still except for grim muttering from the basement, and for Shanice, curled up and sobbing on the top of the stoop while Onica hugs her and strokes her hair.

Jamel staggers into the house, looking for his mother, and finds her sitting at the kitchen table, clutching her arms to her chest, rocking back and forth, moaning.

Cautiously he reaches out a hand and touches her shoulder, but she shows no sign of recognition. He sinks into a chair. The concrete is spreading through his body, making him heavy, so heavy.

* * *

More sirens swell in the night. For lack of any other thing to do, Mitchell runs. Into Brooklyn Heights now, with its calm tree-lined streets and patrician brownstones—a lit window in a below-street-level apartment provides a curiously unshielded glimpse of someone's living room as he careens past.

A faint, unidentifiable fluttering rises in the night. Mitchell's joints jar as he bounds up off the asphalt onto the hard concrete of the sidewalk. He tugs the front of his T-shirt away from his sweaty chest. The fluttering grows into a hard, insistent thropping: somewhere above, a helicopter, a giant dragonfly, is searching the night.

Panicked anew, he swerves, loses his footing, and sprawls out on the ground.

"Hey buddy, you okay?" A late-night dog walker emerges into the light of a streetlamp, his little white pet straining at the leash.

Mitchell glances down at his scraped, raw palms; looks up in fear. He climbs to his feet and staggers off again, each breath a struggle.

* * *

Somewhere two hundred feet below a man is on the run.

The helicopter pilot steers toward the massed towers of the Wysocki Houses, roars above their yellow security vapor lights. Below, in a playground at the edge of the projects, the shadow of a jungle gym swings wildly under his searchlight. A crew of homeboys glares up into the false sun.

A block on, three squad cars and an ambulance converge in a side street, flashing beetles surrounding a carcass. Neighbors flow toward the spectacle. It's hard for the pilot to see down through the summer leaves, but in a cement front yard he can make out two paramedics standing next to a stretcher. A cop guarding the gate looks up and points west.

The radio crackles over the thropping of the rotor blades. "Dispatch to Unit Three-six-eight—be advised: the suspect last sighted bearing north from Court Street and Atlantic Avenue."

The pilot heads toward the East River. He swoops past the bright-lit monolith of the Brooklyn House of Detention where—unless he escapes or gets himself shot—the perp will wind up at the end of this bad night.

The streets of Brooklyn Heights are nearly deserted. Luxury cars, elegant brownstones with glowing bay windows, someone walking a little white dog—only a panicked amateur would flee here.

In the corner of the pilot's eye, a flash of motion. Below, a sprinting figure trips and sprawls in the street. It rises and limps on.

"This is A R-Three-six-eight," the pilot says into his headset, "I'm over Remsen Street between Henry and Hicks: I've got our runner."

* * *

The helicopter throbs overhead and a ray of light slashes down over the block. Sirens sound all around Mitchell. He whirls in terror until he realizes there are no police cars about—the percussive turbulence of the copter blades is setting off car alarms along the street.

He charges across the sidewalk onto a slate path and stops when he discovers his mistake: just ahead of him lies the iron railing of the Promenade, a long walkway overlooking the East River. He looks back to see a police car flashing toward him. There's nothing for it but to plow ahead, out onto the shadowy walk.

Far off, at the other end, another squad car swerves out and skids to a halt.

Mitchell runs.

"This is the police," crackles a loud mechanical voice behind him. "Lay down and put your hands on top of your head."

He runs another ten yards until fear and exhaustion swamp him and he falls to his knees. Moaning, gasping for breath, he looks up through the railing to see Manhattan rising across the dark river, its radiant towers shimmering in the night.

CHAPTER THIRTY-ONE

AFTER THE AMBULANCE HAS GONE, THE POLICE HAVE GONE, THE party guests have gone; after Shanice has been taken back to the projects by her mother; after listening to his own mother keening into the early morning hours, Jamel lies in bed, tortured by the memory of his daughter splayed across the sidewalk, by the weight of her limp body in his arms. Finally, twisting the sheets, he falls asleep, gripped by a strange dark dream of looking up into the sky over Atlantic Avenue, watching a flock of birds being inexorably drawn into the Brooklyn House of Detention.

* * *

In the morning, Grace sits in her kitchen eating her breakfast egg, her heart churned by an unsettled mixture of gladness and shock—gladness over Charles's return, shock over last night's news. A terrible fascination compels her to rise and move through the house to the front window, to see if Jamel Wilson will emerge from his house to enact his usual ritual of hosing down the walk.

* * *

At midday Kristin, sitting on a hard bench in the visitor's waiting room of the House of Detention, takes out a tissue and wipes her raw, swollen eyelids. Then she presses her hands against her belly, feeling for a sign of her growing baby.

* * *

Late in the afternoon, Carol kneels in a corner of her garden, pulling weeds away from the base of a rose bush. A sound startles her and she looks up: it's just the orange cat scrambling over the fence. Across the courtyard, her neighbor Grace emerges from her garden shed. They stare at each other for a moment, but don't speak. Carol turns away. It seems to her that—after all these years—they really don't have much in common.

* * *

As the sky over the rooftops fades, as the air grays in the invisible smoke of dusk, the show begins. A splash of yellow flares along a chain-link fence. With a silent *Pop!* a second primrose opens, then another, like a tiny fireworks show, like a world of possibilities sparking in the fading light.

ACKNOWLEDGMENTS

I would like to thank a number of folks who helped make this book possible.

A couple of people championed it from its earliest days. Thanks to Lisa Bankoff and, most especially, Miriam Cohen, who believed in this book even at times when its own author's faith faltered.

I thank Monroe Cohen, who taught me to love justice and mercy.

My fond appreciation to a trio of consultants who kindly made their expertise available: Tim Cross, for sports; Jared C. (a.k.a. Master Chan), for hip-hop; and Paula M. Kimper, for her gardening genius. (Any errors are mine alone.) Thanks also to Wende Persons and BJ Fredricks, neighbors (and gardeners) par excellence. Thanks to James Wilcox and Sheila Kohler, for good writing advice, and to Rosie Cubero, for sharing the intricacies of office life. Grateful thanks to Mary Gannett, Henry Zook, and Zack Zook for their continuing support of me and many other Brooklyn writers.

Thanks to the late Gladys Johnson, for her inspiring integrity and dignity.

I would like to offer my heartfelt gratitude to Jordan and Anita Miller, Sarah Olson (for the superb design), Jacob Schroeder, and everyone else at Academy Chicago Publishers for making this book a reality.

Finally, I would like to thank S. for blasting his music, driving me to distraction, and providing the germ of this novel. *When life gives you lemons, make lemonade.*